parABnormal Magazine

March 2025

Edited by H. David Blalock

parABnormal Magazine
March 2025

All rights reserved. No part of this book may be reproduced or transmitted in any form or by any means, electronic or mechanical, including photocopying or recording or by any information storage and retrieval systems, without expressed written consent of the authors and/or artists.

parABnormal Magazine is a work of fiction. Names, characters, places, and incidents are products of the authors' imaginations. Any resemblance to actual events or persons, living or dead, is entirely coincidental.

Story and illustration copyrights owned by the respective authors and artists.

>Cover illustration by Mat Kaminski
>Cover design by Laura Givens
>First Printing, March 2025
>Hiraeth Publishing http://www.hiraethsffh.com/

"The Bizarre Sis-Boom-Bah of *Bride of the Gorilla*" originally published in *The Hatchet: The Journal of Lizzie Borden Studies,* April 2015

Vol. VII, No. 1, Issue 25   March 2025

parABnormal Magazine is published quarterly on the 15th day of March, June, September, and December in the United States of America by Hiraeth Publishing, P.O. Box 1248, Tularosa, NM, 88352. ©2025 by Hiraeth Publishing. Nothing may be reproduced in whole or in part without written permission from the authors and artists. Any similarity between places and persons mentioned in the fiction or semi-fiction and real places or persons living or dead is coincidental. Writers and artists guidelines are available online at www.hiraethsffh.com. Guidelines are also available upon request from Hiraeth Publishing, P.O. Box 1248, Tularosa, NM, 88352, if request is accompanied by a self-addressed #10 envelope with a first-class US stamp. Editor: H. David Blalock.

Contents

Stories
6	Foretastes of the Grave by Robert J. Krog
22	Missing You by Sophia Adamowicz
34	Winds of Acolus by Susan E. Rogers
53	Them Boogers Will Get Y'all by Ginger Strivelli
59	Thanks for the Memories by Mike Murphy
73	The Man with Red Hands by A.K. McCarthy
88	An Old Fireplace by Jade Jiao

Poems
21	Fearwood by Freya Pickard
33	The Visitor by A J Dalton
51	Tylwyth Teg by Christian Dickinson
58	The Girl Who Fed On Nightmares by A.A. Alhaji
72	The Sacred Cats of Burma by Lavinia Kumar
87	Doppelgängers by Simon MacCulloch

Articles
99	Treating the Supernatural, the Mysterious, the Occult, and the Weird with the writings of Arthur Machen...by Sonali Roy
106	The Bizarre Sis-Boom-Bah of *Bride of the Gorilla by* Denise Noe
115	*Polyvagal theory: a Potentially Unifying Conceptual Framework for Paranormal Experiences* by R.D. Hayes

Illustrations
86	Abandoned by Sonali Roy
98	Untitled by Naomi Sheely

A Little Help, Please

In the world of the small indie press we fight a never-ending battle for attention to our work, as writers and in publishing. Here's an example: big publishers [you know who they are] have gobs of $$$ that they can devote to advertising and marketing. Here at Hiraeth Publishing, our advertising budget consists of the deposits for whatever soda bottles and aluminum cans we can find alongside the highways. Anti-littering laws make our task even more difficult . . . 9

That's where YOU come in. YOU are our best promoter. YOU are the one who can tell others about us. Just send 'em to our website, tell them about our store. That's all. Just that.

Of course, we don't mind if you talk us up. We're pretty good, you know. We have some award-winning and award-nominated writers and artists, plus other voices well-deserving to be heard [not everyone wins awards, right?] but our publications are read-worthy nevertheless.

That number once again is:

www.hiraethsffh.com

Friend us on Facebook at Hiraeth Publishing

Follow us on Twitter at @HiraethPublish1

What???
No subscription to
parABnormal Magazine??

We can fix that . . .
Just go here and order:
https://www.hiraethsffh.com/product-page/parabnormal-magazine-subscription

or scan

*...also makes a great gift
any time of the year*

Foretastes of the Grave
Robert J. Krog

"This knife, sharpened like a razor, for the butchering of cattle and pigs, used by Hocar yesterday to slit his rival's throat, was found in a blackberry bush near the bog, wet with Laga's blood."

Gelth raised it up for the jury and all beheld it under the early spring sun. Hocar nudged his advocate. Goa stood and stepped across the grass to be recognized by the judge. Given his turn, he spoke, as was his obligation.

"The knife is bloody, but we don't know if it's Laga's blood or a cow's."

Gelth nodded. "That's true, but Laga was found in the bog with his throat slit. Hocar was seen leaving the bog and the blackberry bush just before Laga and the knife were found. He was seen walking there with Laga shortly before."

"There was sufficient time for any number of things to have happened. Hocar says he left Laga there alive. He thinks a child took the knife to play and threw it in the bush when an adult came by. There were several children hunting for frogs by the bog earlier in the morning. I suggest to the jury that we can't know what happened to Laga. There simply isn't sufficient evidence to say Hocar did anything wrong. Wanting the same girl isn't murder. Laga had others with grudges against him."

"Your objections are noted," said Nath from the judge's chair. "Please sit."

Gelth continued, "Hocar had blood on his sleeves, and whatever he may have said to explain it, it was too fresh to have come from his visit to the butcher earlier in the day. It's true no one saw him do the deed, but he'd been quarreling with Laga off and on for days, had threatened him the day before, and was the last person seen alive with Laga before he was killed. There were no other footprints around except those of children. I don't see how the jury cannot proclaim his guilt."

Hocar elbowed Goa again, but his advocate ignored him. He dug the elbow in harder, and Goa hissed under his breath. "We've said it already. There's nothing left. The jury will decide."

Gelth spoke for another few minutes, reviewing, reiterating, and showing the bloodstained knife. Nearby, in Laga's parent's house, his body was being prepared for burial, and the sound of weeping could be heard. Gelth sat down. Nath rose. "Before the Jury decides, advocate for the accused, have you any final statement?"

Goa froze. Hocar whispered fiercely to him. "Say something. I'm innocent. Say something."

Goa rose. Seeming at a loss, he cleared his throat and looked around. The Jury, dressed in their soberest grays, sitting with their backs to bushes in bloom with delicate, pink flowers and brilliant evergreen trees, waited expectantly for him, white haired men and women with more summers and winters behind them than Hocar could really imagine. Their faces were appropriately impassive. Hocar prayed, hardly able to hear his own voice in his head over the pounding of his heart. His temples had begun to throb. *Dear Jesus, don't let me be found guilty. I'll do anything. I'll never harm another person. I'll become a monk. I'll never look at a female. I'll pray for sinners every day til I die. Don't let them proclaim my guilt.*

Goa breathed deeply. "Hocar contends he's innocent. He has no explanation for what happened to Laga, only a theory. He says he walked with Laga out of the village discussing the love of Juriga, trying to convince his friend that the girl was not for him. They argued, and Hocar left him there by the bog, unharmed. They had been friends since childhood. Just because he can't explain what happened, doesn't mean he's at fault. Laga was always a quarrelsome boy. There were others in the village who had grudges and could have exploited the situation. Gelth has called witnesses for their whereabouts, but some of them had only their own word for alibis. Doesn't that cast enough doubt on the situation?"

Hocar bowed his head into his hands. Hearing it, he wouldn't have believed it. Goa spoke for another minute, but Hocar didn't listen. When Goa sat again, Nath rose and instructed all but the Jury to pick up their chairs and leave the lawn, while the jury formed a circle for their discussion. They did so, and Hocar found himself quickly abandoned, carrying his chair back to his house alone and setting it before the door. He looked around and saw that his grandmother and brother were not around. Then he fled to the chapel to pray again his hopeless, guilty prayer before the tabernacle.

A quarter of an hour later, Nath was at the chapel door, calling him out into the village square. He dried his eyes, crossed himself, rose, and walked out from the dimmer, candlelit, incensed interior into the bright, fresh air under the blue sky of spring. Everyone he knew, from his brother and grandmother to the few in the village he was not related to were gathered. The mutual friends with whom he and Laga had played and learned as children were there together with Laga's brother, Jeb. Juriga and her parents were on the other side. Her eyes avoided him. Her wheat-colored hair covered most of her face, her youthful, supple, blossoming body turned partly away from him.

Nath stepped out from the others, fists enclosing a declaration of guilt or innocence. "Accused, come forward."

With hesitant steps, he advanced to the judge. Nath raised his hands over Hocar's head, sprinkling crushed, dead oak leaves over him. "You are found guilty and sentenced to die by the method with which you slew your friend. By these, you are restrained until the executioner arrives."

He stumbled back from the judge, unable to breath, his labored heart still thudding, his temples throbbing deafeningly. He fell, sitting on the hard-packed earth, and tried frantically to brush the bits of dead leaves out of his hair and off his clothes, but they clung. The light in his eyes changed. Colors became drabber, browner, grayer, dimmer. Shadows became blacker. The sunlight cooled. The smells of spring receded to a dusty odor. All sounds seemed further away.

"No," he said.

His suddenly drab neighbors turned away, going about their business, their shadows, long and distorted, following them with jerky motions. They had a murdered man to bury and mourn, a family to comfort. His numb hands kept trying to brush the brown flakes away, rearranging them, but never succeeding. He cast about for some better means of removing them and saw the shadows of buildings were rippling, writhing. Eventually, he flung himself face down on the ground and lay there with his clothes covering his head.

Later, when the sun was higher in the gray sky and the air should have been warmer, he heard footsteps and raised his head furtively to see who it might be. His brother and grandmother approached from the direction of Laga's parent's house. Their shadows were mostly in order, only a little indistinct on the edges. His head fell to the dirt, and thus he lay.

"My boy, my son's son. I have prayed and prayed for you, and I am so ashamed for you."

He kept his eyes on their feet.

"Have you nothing to say?"

There was a hole in his brother's left shoe.

"Laga was our friend," said his brother. "Juriga was free to choose whom she would. You couldn't respect that?"

He closed his eyes. His grandmother wept. Their footsteps receded. Another set approached. Maybe it was Juriga. He peeked. It was Jeb. He closed his eyes. Very close, Jeb spoke.

"It'll be justice, and I'll watch. The executioner will be here soon."

Jeb, too, left.

The executioner will slit my throat, and I will die grasping at it and thrashing, the light in my eyes fading. Jeb will watch for many breaths and be satisfied. I would do the same. It will be fast but feel long, and then I will be dead.

He rolled over, his eyes sweeping the gray sky. *I am made harmless and helpless. I have to live like this, with foretastes of death until he arrives.*

Behind him, the chapel bell rang, still large, round, and resonant. His prayer had not been answered. Bitterness filled his mouth, and he screamed. Rage took him, and he pounded the ground with his fists and feet until they hurt. The bell finished tolling noon. He wept.

Is this what Hell is like? Am I half there already? Is the next change that this drab world catches fire? Does all fade, and I burn? Will I see the other damned souls, or will I be alone?

He wished Father Alby were there to ask where the mercy of God was. But their village was on a circuit, and Father Alby was away. Unable to lay there any longer, he picked his aching body up and stood with eyes downcast to avoid the twisting, rippling shadows but saw his own. It was a horror, not human but like a gargoyle, with oversized, misshapen head, jutting spikes, and a tail. His mouth was huge.

"That can't be me."

He averted his eyes and limped away across to his house for some food, his traveling cloak, and his walking stick. Father Alby would answer him. He gathered what he needed, opening and leaving open the cupboard, his one chest, the shutters, and the door. Jeb met him there.

"Running?" Laga's brother asked.

Without a word, he limped past him and down the street, heading out north. When he was a mile away, Jeb, with his hat, stick, and pack, caught up.

"What are you doing?" he asked, too despondent to be harsh or hateful.

"I told you I'm going to see the justice done. Where you are, I will be."

They walked the rest of the day. In the warm afternoon, Jeb shed his cloak, and Hocar did too, though he did not feel hot. They spoke no words between them, but as night fell and Hocar turned off the road to ask for shelter at a farmhouse known for being hospitable to travelers, Jeb asked, "Do you think to avoid the Executioner? He'll find you wherever you go. The crushed oak leaves mark you for what you are, and he'll home in on them like a bat to a gnat."

"I'm not running from but to," he said.

"You're going the wrong way. The executioner comes from the west. If you wish to hasten the end." Jeb left it hanging.

Hocar, his cloak off and over his arm, knocked, and the door was opened by a young man with a little girl clinging to his leg. The girl's curious eyes took him in without understanding, but the man's knew.

"May we sleep in your barn, if it's not too much trouble?"

"I don't know," the young man answered.

"He can't harm anyone, now," Jeb put in.

"But."

"It won't happen here; the summons was only issued at noon."

"Still, he's condemned."

"I can pay," Hocar said.

He hesitated.

"I'm no danger, and I'll pay double what the inn would charge."

The young man looked at Jeb who only shrugged.

"Very well, sleep in the barn. I'll bring you a loaf. There's water in the well. Wait, here's a lantern."

They went to a sturdy, old barn occupied by a brown draft horse and a pair of dark, smallish oxen to make themselves comfortable.

Hocar had tried to look at as little as he could as the shadows lengthened toward sunset. The trees seemed to be reaching out to take hold of him. The shadows of road signs looked like gallows. Boulders cast darknesses like deep pits into which he might fall and never return. Jeb's shadow betrayed a form bloated and clawed. In a way, the fall of night was a grace. Individual shadows blended into one formless darkness, except where the weak lantern light fell. He shut his eyes and waited for their host to bring bread. Jeb took the lantern out to the well and drew water. When he returned, he offered Hocar a cup.

Surprised, he took it. It tasted dry, but he drank.

"The mark changes you?" Jeb asked him.

He said nothing.

Jeb went on as if making conversation, "They say a man marked begins to lose his sight and hearing in this world and to see and hear into the spirit world instead. It's true? Have you already half descended to the dead?"

"It would please you?"

"Please? I'm curious. I think it would satisfy me in a way. It would be a certain, preliminary justice, don't you think?"

He drank more of the dry water and closed his eyes.

"I can see by your expression it's true. I've watched you. You react to things I can't perceive, and you've lost the ability to see what I see, haven't you? It's a beautiful day. It's natural you'd appreciate it less, being concerned about your imminent death, or, alternately, it might grieve you to see it, accentuating what you're to lose. You might curse it. I think you're half in the afterlife already, getting a taste of what's coming to you. Am I wrong?"

Without opening his eyes, he offered, "Why won't you let me be? Stay here until the executioner passes this way pursuing me. Follow him. It's not as if I can escape."

He was answered with soft laughter at the edge of his hearing. Their host's footsteps entered, crunching straw.

"Here's the bread, and my wife sent some cheese as well. Condemned man, she prays for you and urges me to join her, so I will. There are two plates here."

Jeb thanked him, and he left. Hocar kept his eyes closed, grateful he couldn't hear Jeb smacking his lips. Later, he looked and found his plate before him atop the straw on the floor. There was a cat sniffing at it which he shooed away. He took it and ate. The bread seemed coarse and bland, though it should have been soft by how it tore, the cheese heavy and dull.

The cat turned sharply at a sound or movement he didn't note and stared hard into an empty stall. He saw for himself a form in the darkness, blacker and harder than other shadows. From it, a foul stench emanated. It did not move, but waited. As he stared, it seemed to take on a different shape, rather like a man in deep robes holding a staff.

He looked away. The cat continued to stare.

"You see what it sees?" asked Jeb.

He ignored him.

The shadow was there all through the night. Hocar curled up out of sight of it and pretended to sleep, at some point, drifting off. When he woke, Jeb was standing over him, nudging him with his walking stick.

"The sun's up. Where will you flee today?"

"Let me alone. I need to relieve myself."

"Their privy is between the house and the barn."

He rose, pushed past and shook his stiff limbs out as he walked to the privy. The stinking shade in the empty stall was less distinct in the daytime, but somehow more identifiable, a ferryman with a pole, standing in his little boat. When they left, heading north again, it didn't follow, but the world was even duller, grayer, browner, with wan sunlight, shoddy, a poor imitation of all he'd ever known.

When Jeb asked him again what he saw on that fresh, dewy, brilliant morning, he answered, "The colors have faded out, and the shapes are all like a child's doodle. Your shadow is a demon."

He looked at it and realized that it had changed though. While his own was still much like a gargoyle's, Jeb's had eased back into a more manlike shape even if it rippled at the edges and moved with a jerky motion that did not match his actual stride.

"My shadow is a demon? What is yours like?"

"Yours is like a gargoyle. Mine is normal."

Jeb paused and looked hard after him, so he said, "You want me lie?"

A smile crossed Jeb's face. "No, the truth. Why did you kill my brother? Did he attack you? Who started it? Did you plan it?"

The question was unexpected. He quickened the pace.

"Not in a truth telling mood, after all? The executioner will find you tomorrow morning at the latest, you know. You might as well let it out. You can't escape."

They passed the first inn a little later but had no

reason to stop. When the pale, tepid, red ball of the sun reached its apex, they paused under a tree and ate the food they'd brought from home the afternoon before. It more or less assuaged Hocar's hunger, but it was tasteless except for a hint of sour. Jeb enjoyed his hard cheese and rolls.

Out of the silence of hours, Jeb said. "She'd probably have chosen you, not Laga. Goa's right, he was quarrelsome. She dislikes quarreling. He was combative with you because he was losing. Isn't that ironic? You only had to wait, to win. You have, or had, manners. Laga didn't. I understand why you did it. I often wanted to choke him myself, but had you waited, well, you might be betrothed. The women say she was close to making her decision when you cut my brother's throat." He said it plainly, looking Hocar in the eyes.

Hocar knew his face must have flushed. He had no answer.

"You needn't be angry. It's all too late, but I think it's important you know."

"Are you trying to torture me?" he asked. *If I were not restrained by the curse of my sentencing, would I attack him? Would I send him to join Laga?* He balled his fists without thinking about it.

"You aren't dead yet, so there's a chance for wisdom, right?" He laughed then, and began collecting his things. "Where now? Run, or meet the executioner on the way home?"

Hocar gathered his things and walked north, as before.

"Still running away?" Jeb asked.

"Running to."

"To what?"

***

He pushed hard after nightfall to reach the next village. They were footsore but did not go to the inn.

"Where are you taking us, Hocar? It's time for your last dinner. I'll pay for the best the house has."

Hocar went rather to the little rectory beside the church.

"Here? I wonder what you hope for?"

He knocked hard on the door until the priest answered and asked, "What's the emergency?"

"Father Alby," he began, but his voice broke, and he couldn't speak.

"Come in," instructed Father Alby, clearly weary.

Hocar collapsed into a chair in the small, sitting room and threw his cloak open to reveal the clinging leaf fragments.

"I see," said the priest. "Hocar, isn't it? I baptized you, I think."

"Yes, Father," he was sobbing and couldn't stop.

Turning to Jeb, Father Alby said, "I'll find you something to eat. Put your things by the door."

Jeb wanted to say it was a fool's errand, but the words stuck in his throat. He stood by the door, watching Hocar weeping. Momentarily, the priest returned and ushered Jeb into the kitchen where half a baked chicken, bread, and wine awaited. Returning, he took Hocar by the arm to the church, next door. They entered into color. The one red candle by the tabernacle burned. The gold shone beside it, and Hocar gasped.

"Yes, you've murdered a man then, haven't you, my boy?"

"Father."

"Into the confessional, shall we?"

"Where is the mercy of God?" he shouted. "I'm nineteen years old."

"Are you guilty? The mercy of God is in the sacrament, my son." Father Alby pointed at the confessional.

"We quarreled, it's true, but I didn't mean to."

"You murdered him or not?"

He stood there in the church, with the shadowy forms of Saints about him, with the gold of the tabernacle shining and the crucifix above it, looking sadly down. He half turned to run. The priest took him by the arm.

"Hocar, by the grace of your baptism, you murdered

him or not?"

He broke free of the old man's grip, went to the door, opened it, and fell to his knees there between the drab and vivid. Father Alby's hand settled on his shoulder.

"I can't force you to confess, but I urge it. You cannot escape the curse. It is for justice. If you murdered a man, justice it is. I wouldn't have you die, but it is the law. There is a course remaining which saves your soul, confess and do penance, facing justice. The sacraments are for salvation. Come to the confessional."

Hocar looked outside and recoiled. He rose and shut the door.

"Even now, do not despair."

So he went and sat in his side of the shriving pew, Father Alby in the other.

"In the name of the Father, Son, and Holy Ghost, Amen," began Father Alby, and Hocar crossed himself.

"May the Lord be in your heart and help you to confess your sins with true sorrow."

"Father, I don't want to die. I'm nineteen."

"I know, my son. Confess your sins."

At first, nothing came. His throat closed up, and his tongue thickened. His eyes stung.

"Whom are you accused of murdering?"

Phrased that way, he could answer. "Laga."

"I remember Laga."

"Yes."

"You quarreled?"

"Yes."

"Over?"

"We." He could get no further.

"Property? A girl?"

"A girl, Father."

"Juriga?"

"How?"

"Lucky guess. Go on. Why accuse you?"

It began to feel very hot in the confessional. He pulled his cloak off. The leaves crinkled.

"Go on, Hocar."

"He was found in the bog with his throat slit by a

knife stolen from the butcher."

"Murder or self defense or accident?"

"I took it for self defense, Father. I didn't mean to hurt him."

"You thought he'd attack, and you wanted protection. I understand. What happened though?"

"He was insulting. He said Juriga gave him favors, kisses and views of her bosom. He said I should withdraw my suit."

"Go on."

"He turned his back, as if I were nothing, like an arrogant lord, dismissive." Hocar saw it again, Laga sneering and turning his back, his straw-colored hair flicking over his face, folding his arms, looking into the distance as if he had more important things on his mind. "I hated him. I knew he was lying. He had to be, but I feared, just then, that maybe she had. I burned for her. She's all I ever wanted, She'd once promised we'd be together. We were much younger then, but I knew she'd meant it. The thought of her lying, of him seeing her intimately, kissing her, was too much. He had his chin high up, acting like a lord, so I stepped close behind and cut his throat. He fell. It was horrible. He kept trying to breathe, but couldn't. His eyes were so desperate. But I was afraid. I couldn't help him, so I shoved him into the bog and ran."

He was finished and didn't know what else to say. Father Alby was quiet on the other side of the curtain. He realized he was weeping again.

"Did you want to save him?" Father Alby's voice was calm.

"I don't know. I wish I had now."

"Are you sorry for this sin and all those associated with it and any other sins you have committed since last I heard your confession?"

He thought a moment, and the shame overtook him. He was sorry, and it wracked him. His brother was right. Laga had been their friend. They'd known each other all their lives.

"Yes, Father, I'm sorry." It was hard to speak as the

anger changed to contrition.

"Have you any other sins to tell me?"

"In the last month, I have told countless lies trying to impress others, especially Juriga, and I have lusted for her."

"You are sorry?"

"Yes, Father." He felt broken. Every part of him ached. His face, and hands, and sleeves, and the shelf on which he rested his elbows were wet with his tears.

"For you penance, say your act of contrition, and express your sorrow to all you have offended as the opportunity arises before the executioner arrives."

he said, somehow,"Oh, my God, I am sorry for my sins with all my heart. In choosing to do evil and failing to do good, I have sinned against you whom I should love above all things. With your help, I firmly intend to do my penance, to sin no more, and to avoid whatever leads me to sin. Our Savior, Jesus Christ, suffered and died for us. In His name, Lord have mercy."

"God, the Father of mercies, through the death and resurrection of His Son, has reconciled the world to himself and sent the Holy Ghost among us for the forgiveness of sins; through the ministry of the church, may God give you pardon and peace, and I absolve you from your sins in the name of the Father, and Son, and Holy Ghost."

"Amen."

"Go in peace."

He heard the old priest exit the confessional, but he found he could not move.

"Hocar, it is time to come out."

"I'm afraid."

"I'm sure your friend will also want to confess, unless he came with no heart for vengeance. Fetch him here."

So commanded, he exited the shriving pew and went out into the dark, making his way on stumbling feet to the rectory.

Jeb was in the cozy kitchen at the table with the red and white checked cloth, finishing his meal. He looked up, appraised Hocar's wrecked face, and smiled crookedly. "There's enough left for you, if you like. It's not the fine last meal I'd have bought you, but it's something, unless you want to go to the inn."

"Father wants you in the church."

"Let's go then."

He said fast before the words stuck, "I'm sorry I murdered Laga."

Jeb rose and hit him under his left eye, above his jaw. He went down, stunned. Distantly, he heard "Rot in Hell," and a foot stepped on him. The door clattered shut.

On the floor, his head swimming among stars, hardly cognizant of the pain yet, he realized the colors had come back. Struggling, he got up and looked around dim room. The shadows were normal shadows, flickering only with the candle flame and the glow from the hearth. The statue of Mother Mary was blue and white, and her eyes brown. The roses around here were red and yellow. He brushed his hands over his clothes. The dried, dead, oak leaves were still there.

Outside, horses' hooves sounded on the cobbled stones, and cart wheels rumbled on them. A resonant male voice called, "Hocar, come out."

"Who is it?" But he knew.

"I am the executioner, Hocar. Come forth."

It was useless to run. Knowing his penance, he went out. The executioner was a medium sized man, hooded so his face was invisible. He sat atop a plain, unadorned cart pulled by plain, sturdy horses.

"I can see the colors again. I hear and smell. I'm not half in the land of death anymore."

"That is an encouraging sign, but it does not mitigate the punishment, and if you look, you may see you are partly there."

He looked up, and there were stars, clear, icy, and so far away, but splendid. They'd never been brighter.

"The glory of creation. If you appreciate it, I give you a moment."

Hocar dropped his eyes and caught sight of another man stepping out from churchyard, a caretaker perhaps.

Light from a window illuminated him, and he nodded solemnly. Hocar returned the nod. The executioner's eyes flicked that way and back curiously. "Are you ready?"

"I'm afraid." He shook.

"It will only be a moment. You are shriven?"

"Yes."

"Climb into the cart."

He walked that way, having to pass the caretaker, and the man took his arm and asked, "How does that headstone read?"

Hocar looked, and there was enough light. "Lord, you know all things; you know that I love you."

The man released him, and he climbed up, tripping. The executioner caught him. They stepped to the middle of the cart.

"This is the knife you used to slit your friend's throat."

Hocar's eyes bulged.

"Tell my family I repented."

He nodded. "Are you ready?" The man's face, visible at the last, was that of a kind uncle. For a moment, Hocar hoped it would not happen, but the eyes were steady of purpose.

"Lord have mercy on me, a sinner."

The executioner cut his throat.

It stung like fire, and he would have said so. The blood rushed into his throat and windpipe, and the last air left his lungs for good. He fell to his knees, blood soaking his shirt and down his pants. He fell over on the bed of the cart. His eyes cast desperately about for succor and beheld the stars, and he would have asked if they were stars or angels, but his vision faded, and he had no voice.

***

The executioner was wrapping Hocar's corpse for travel and burial. Looking up, he saw Father Alby kneeling and praying for the repose of Hocar's soul, Jeb standing white faced and confused.

"Father, he was shriven? He said he was. I intend to

see him buried in his own place, if so."

When he was done praying, Father Alby said, "He was."

"Even a murder may make a good end. Who is this?" He pointed at Jeb.

"They were neighbors."

"Need a ride home, lad?" The executioner asked.

Numbly, Jeb joined him on the cart.

Fearwood
Freya Pickard

Beyond the clustered trunks of bone
Beyond the withered roots of stone
Beyond the ivy, shrivelled, bare
There stands a clearing - will you dare
To step beyond the sacred ash
To raise your head, the question ask
To wait beneath the swaying corpse
To look into the whitened eye
Of blank unknowing, I am I
And comprehend the sacrifice
Of nine times nine in wind and ice?

Missing You
Sophia Adamowicz

Last night, I waited—as always—for the tread of your footsteps down the corridor.

I'm so used to them now that I can mimic the heavy sound of one foot and the lazy drag of the other.

Thump, scrape. Near the top of the stairs.

Thump, scrape. Passing Mum's bedroom, passing the window and the antique side table and the place where the floorboard dips and causes you to stumble and —

Thump, scrape. Outside my room.

The first time I heard it, the thrashing of my heart made the bed sheets tremble. The whole world shrank to the gap under my door and the two patches of thick darkness where, I was sure, you'd planted your feet. The doorknob was a frozen O. But how long would it be frozen? What if it turned and the latch... clicked?

As the weeks went by, fear turned into familiarity. Familiarity became a strange sort of comfort.

You kept a respectful distance.

I even used to bid you goodnight. You were only patrolling, after all—checking that I was safely tucked into bed, giving me more attention than Mum does now that her journeys to and from work take so long. By the time she gets home, she's too tired to talk to me properly about the new school. At least I had you, my guardian spirit.

Then, last night, I waited. And you didn't come.

***

It's been a week.

"You look tired, Kay," says Mum, leaning against the kitchen counter.

I'm surprised she's noticed. Then again, it's taking me longer to get dressed in the morning. I eat breakfast so slowly that the cornflakes bloat and break apart. I'd have thought that waiting up all night in case you showed up would boost my appetite, not kill it off.

"I'm fine."

Setting down her mug, she stands on tiptoe and reaches up to the top shelf of the cupboard, her blouse coming untucked from her skirt.

"Here," she says, handing me a see-through container of multivitamins with iron. The pills are huge and brown, like pellets of eco-friendly cat litter.

"I don't need them."

She grunts. "Up to you."

"Like I said, I'm fine."

"Okay, okay." Tucking her shirt in, she grabs her bag and car keys. "Don't be late for school."

"I'm never late."

"Hm."

Mum's face disappears behind the large mug of coffee. She must've poured it a while ago; the heat-sensitive picture of her and me on holiday in Spain has already started to turn black as the drink cools.

"I'll see you later then, all right?" she says after she's drained the dregs. Her tired eyes find mine. "We can order a pizza."

Here it is, the olive branch. The *forgive-me-for-not-being-around* bribe. "I thought I was lacking essential vitamins? Pizzas don't have much nutritional value."

She breaks off her gaze. "Whatever, Kaylee. It's up to you. I just wish that sometimes you'd see what's good for you."

"Like what? Dominos?"

With another grunt, she leaves. I push away what's left of my cereal and sit alone at the breakfast table until the hands of the clock creep past nine.

You weren't a dream or imaginary. I heard you every single night.

What happened to you?

Ghosts don't just go missing—do they?

I look it up online.

Ghost disappearing only brings up articles and stories about spirits walking through walls or vanishing before someone's eyes. I type, *How to get a ghost to come back* and get hundreds of sites telling me how to deal with a girlfriend or boyfriend who's ignoring my messages. Funny that there's nothing about being ghosted by an actual ghost.

But some instinct tells me to keep going, onto the second, and then the third page of results. That's when I find her: Mabs Hicklin.

The website looks like it was made at a time when no-one really knew what the internet was. The links to different parts of the site all appear in a blue list down the left-hand side, and there are no pictures of Mabs herself. I click on the 'About' section.

Edinburgh-born Mabs Hicklin is a mystic, medium and professional endorcist or 'ghost re-homer.' As the name implies, an endorcist is the opposite of an exorcist, in that the process involves inviting spiritual presences into the human realm rather than driving them out of it. Working closely with those who wander beyond the veil, Mabs has successfully re-located over 70 untethered spirits. Both the living and the dead rate her services highly (see Testimonials).

I click on the link to the 'Testimonials' page and read rave reviews from average-looking pubs that are now graced with a ghostly presence. '*Customers flock to hear the footsteps crossing the Green Room!*' one hotel manager boasts. There are also some photographs of Ouija boards which have apparently spelt out 'Thank you' from re-homed spirits.

It seems ludicrous, impossible. But I find myself dialing the number at the top of the webpage.

***

The woman at the door is broad-shouldered and squat. Beneath her fedora hat, mushroom-coloured hair frizzes out in all directions.

"Kaylee Fisher?" Her voice has a Scottish lilt.

"Yes," I say. "Come in."

Mum would go mad if she knew I was inviting a stranger into the house, never mind a stranger who claims to work with spirits wandering beyond the veil. At least she wipes her leather boots on the welcome mat.

"Beautiful place," she says, looking up at the

wooden beams. "Late sixteenth century, I presume?"

I nod, impressed. "The estate agent said 1590s."

"Been here long?"

"No. We moved here just over two months ago."

"And you're looking for a tenant?"

"A tenant?"

She grins. Her teeth are spaced a little too far apart, as if she grew up with a coin lodged between each of them.

"Of the supernatural kind, I mean."

"Oh, not exactly. It's more complicated than that... Would you like a cup of tea?"

"Nah, I've got this." She pats a Thermos flask tucked into the side pocket of her rucksack. "Hot Toddy—nectar of the gods. My Nan used to make it when I was a wee thing. Not much was known about the effect it had on a developing brain back then. More innocent times. In case you're wondering, it's diluted whisky, flavoured with sugar and cinnamon."

"Sounds nice," I say, though the one time I tried whisky, I hated the stuff.

"Come on. Let's sit down together, eh, and you can explain why you called."

She walks through to the living room as if she already knows exactly where everything is, and makes herself comfortable on the sofa. While she pours herself a Hot Toddy, I tell her about you: when I first became aware of you; how you went on a nightly patrol at 11:45pm for a couple of months; and how you stopped, abruptly, last week.

"So you see it as protective, do you, this spirit?" The fug of whisky drifts from Mabs's steaming flask lid. She can't use very much water in that recipe.

"Like a guardian angel, kind of."

"And what makes you think this spirit *wants* to come back, Kaylee?"

I knit my fingers together, staring into the enormous fireplace that made Mum so excited when we first viewed this place.

"He seemed to be looking out for me, you know? Like, this is something he used to do when he was alive.

Maybe he was a father."

"He? You think it's the ghost of a man?"

I try not to look at the photo on the mantelpiece. A complete family. Mum, me and Dad.

"I'm not sure."

A silence thickens between us. She seems to be waiting for me to break it, but I don't know what to say. Eventually, she speaks.

"Have you ever watched a David Attenborough documentary?"

I frown. "You mean, the old guy who talks about the planet?"

"That's the one. He's often accused of anthropomorphising animals. Making them sound human, you know."

"Okay...?" Has she really come here to talk about what's on TV?

"My point is, we make a lot of assumptions about things that are different from us. We assign them motivations that we, as living human beings, can understand. But ghosts, like animals, belong to a different order of things."

"Ghosts are people," I say. "Only, they're people who've died, aren't they?"

Mabs's lips form an upside-down U. "Some of them."

I can't help but shudder at her words.

"I don't care what he is," I say, fighting down a growing sense of unease. "Just bring him back, please."

She unzips the rucksack, takes out a black notebook bristling with index tabs and flicks through it. "Never had a job like this before—asking a ghost to return to the same place. Usually, they've been banished by an exorcist and can't get back to where they've come from, poor things, so they wander round until I re-home them in some country pub or a stately home a few miles off."

"But do you think you can do it?"

"Here we go." She taps the page in her notebook. It's a drawing of a circle with a squiggly pattern, a bit like a hook, inside it. "I'll give it my best shot. First, though, we need to see if we can make contact. The spirit may still be lurking around here, even if it's gone quiet."

***

The kitchen table is the best place for the Ouija board. Mabs lays it out, along with a pointer that looks like a guitar plectrum. A *planchette*, she calls it. The object has a hole through the top so that we can see what letter of the alphabet it lands on.

"Make yourself comfortable," she says, scraping back a chair. "Then put your index and middle finger on the planchette."

For a moment, I hesitate. What if you don't make contact? What if all this is a momentous waste of time and money?

But what if it isn't? Mabs might be the one person who can help me get you back.

I pull up a chair and place my fingers on the planchette, next to hers.

Mabs clears her throat and takes a few deep breaths. My own breathing falls into the same slow rhythm. It startles me when she finally says, "Spirit! I, Mabs Hicklin, and resident of this house, Kaylee Fisher, call upon you to make contact. If you're here with us, let us know by moving the planchette over to 'Yes' on the board."

I wait for a force to move the object under my cold and trembling fingers.

Nothing.

Mabs repeats the question.

Still nothing.

I look up. Mabs's pale pink tongue is poking out of the side of her mouth, and her forehead is creased in thought.

"What do we do now?" I whisper.

"Hmm. Looks like we'll have to get straight onto the summoning. Why don't you show me where it walks, eh?"

I lead Mabs upstairs to the long corridor where I used to hear the sound of your footfall. In the daytime, the dark wooden floorboards and criss-cross beams in the walls don't look so oppressive.

As she draws the symbol from the black book onto the floor, all I can think about is whether it's going to be easy to get chalk marks off wood.

"Parents know you're doing this?" Mabs asks, as if reading my mind.

"No. But I can pay you in full, if you're worrying about that. I do pet sitting."

"I'm not worrying about the money."

When she's finished, she sits on her heels and rubs the small of her back. "Hard on the spine, this is. And the knees." She looks over her shoulder at me. "You go off downstairs and have a cup of tea during the next bit, Kaylee."

"Why?"

"It's not for you to see."

My stomach twists. I've invited this utterly bizarre stranger into the house. She could do anything up here while I'm not watching—ransack the place, steal my mum's jewellery or my laptop.

"I won't be too long," says Mabs. "Then I'll come and join you downstairs at the Ouija board, and we can have a chat with your, er, chappie."

She turns her back on me. I'm dismissed.

If I want her to summon you, I have no choice but to trust her and do as I'm told.

I go back down to the kitchen. The packet of multivitamins is still on the side. Mum's trying her best. I was pretty narky with her this morning. All right, it would have been better if she'd applied for another job closer to our new home. But she likes the work, and I can't blame her for the fact that I don't really click with anyone at school. Everyone just knows I'm funny. The kind of person who calls an endorcist to get her ghost back. I swallow one of the huge vitamin pellets with a glass of water and slouch in front of the board.

Thump, scrape.

My head snaps up. *Thump, scrape* across the floor of the upstairs landing.

The glass of water nearly slips out of my hand. I bang it down on the table and place my fingers on the planchette.

"Is… is it you?" I ask, breathless.

The planchette moves like a living thing under my fingers, all the way over to 'Yes.' My heart is lodged in my throat. I cough and force out the words.

"Who are you? Tell me your name."

Again, the planchette moves, buzzing with a peculiar sort of heat, and lands on A. Then it slides across to L. Back over to E, then C. Alec. Not my dad's name. But the spirit is a man, just as I thought.

"Why did you leave, Alec?"

The planchette moves over to M and then U. I know what's coming next.

"Mum? My mum?"

'Yes.'

"What about her?"

There's no answer. The question must be too vague.

"What did she do?"

S-E-N-T-M-E-A-W-A-

A loud bang from upstairs makes me jump. The planchette skids across the table, like someone has yanked it away with a piece of string, and falls off the edge. I half expect it to scuttle across the floor, cockroach-like. But it lies there inert. Dead.

For a while, I'm too dazed to do anything apart from drink the water and listen to Mabs clattering around upstairs. I open the kitchen door a crack. It sounds like she's giving the landing a good scrub now.

"Hello? Mabs?"

The scrubbing stops. "Yeah?"

"Is everything all right?"

"Aye."

I tiptoe up the steps to find Mabs shoving a plastic bag of cleaning stuff into the rucksack. There's no trace of the symbol she drew.

"He spoke to me," I say, feeling a nervous smile flicker across my face.

Mabs's face drops. "Who?"

"Alec. The ghost."

"Using the Ouija board?"

"Yes."

Mabs looks like she's got something important to say, perhaps about me using her board when she wasn't in the room, but she presses her lips together and shrugs her backpack onto her shoulders.

"'Scuse me." Squeezing past, she heads for the stairs. "I'll collect the things from the kitchen and then I'll be off."

"But we haven't finished asking questions, have we?"

"We've done quite enough for today."

"Has something gone wrong?"

At the bottom of the steps, she turns. Her chest is heaving.

"I'm sorry. The process I used was very powerful. I've never done this"—she gestures upstairs—"before. Sorry."

"It's okay. You brought Alec back."

She bites the corner of her lip. "Like I said, the process was very powerful. Strong words. A strong symbol. You may get more activity than before."

"Like what?"

"It's an old place, this. Not just the house. The land. It's busy."

"But we're miles from anywhere," I laugh. That's the whole reason why Mum has to travel so far into work. Busy is the opposite of life in this village.

Mabs nods slowly and goes into the kitchen to pick up the rest of her equipment. She's heading for the door before I can even go digging around in my bedroom for the money.

"Don't leave without your payment!"

"No charge," she calls as she leaves.

***

"You think you'll make it into school tomorrow?" Mum asks.

I finish my fourth slice of pizza and nod. "I'm feeling better now. I took a multivitamin, like you said, though I'm pretty sure it's not a deficiency."

"What do you think it is then?"

The mumble of the radio fills the pause.

I shrug. "I don't know. I've not been sleeping well."

"Me neither," says Mum, a bit too quickly.

All this time, I've been thinking I'm the only one who experienced the noises. What if I was never alone in this?

"Have you heard anything... weird in the house?"

Mum freezes with the glass halfway to her lips. "Like what?" she replies with a lightness of tone so forced, it's as obvious as a scream.

"I don't know. Bumps in the night?"

"Why? Have you?"

"It's an old house. There's bound to be creaky floorboards."

I drop my gaze to the nearly empty, grease-stained pizza box, which is resting in the exact same spot as the Ouija board earlier today. The whole experience seems as surreal as a fever dream.

"Well," says Mum, "if there was anything, I'd tell it to leave us in peace."

She takes a sip of wine.

"And you think it'd listen to you?"

"I can be quite persuasive when I want to be." She pushes the last slice of pizza towards me.

S-E-N-T-M-E-A-W-A-

I've been thinking about it all afternoon. Now, finally, it clicks into place. The last letter would be a Y. 'Sent me away.'

Mum made you go, didn't she, Alec?

"You don't need to protect me," I tell her. "I'm perfectly capable of looking after myself."

***

Tonight, I wait—as always—for the tread of your footsteps down the corridor.

My ears pick up every sound. Mum's snores shake the timbers for the first time since we moved here. Outside, a December wind stirs the bare branches of our garden. On a nearby road, a motorbike breaks the speed limit.

Then, another noise, at the top of the stairs.

Thump, scrape. Thump, scrape.

That's what I expect, hope, to hear. But the sound tonight is different. It's less of a step and a drag, and more of a patter. Like something with too many legs.

It walks past my Mum's room without breaking the rhythm of her snores.

"Alec?" I whisper. "Alec, is that you?"

It passes the window, where Mabs drew her symbol today, where a loud bang shook the floor. What caused that? She never explained. It happened just before the planchette flew off the table. It cut off your message, as if something interrupted or, somehow, displaced you.

"Alec?"

What was it Mab said? The process was powerful. It's *busy* around here. I picture the symbol on the floor glowing like firelight, drawing the wandering spirits from this old, old land through the walls, up through the cracks floorboards, into the corridor outside my room.

Past the side table.

I want to scream for Mum, but my body won't move, not a single muscle of it.

A scrambling of feet. It must be at the place where the floorboard dips.

Ghosts are just dead people, aren't they? Some of them, Mabs said. Some of them.

A shadow falls across the gap under my door.

Oh God. What were you guarding me from, Alec?

The doorknob begins to turn.

The Visitor
A J Dalton

He appears sometimes–almost–
as if there's a continuity in his reality:
other times he's not there and that appalls me
more than his stretched visage always
screaming silently, twisting eyes standing out
of his skull, tongue livid, vein worms writhing
clawed hands reaching, preaching, beseeching
his bird screeching, a dream-fluttering corvid
of midnight nightmare gripping his sinewed shoulders
I dare not name him lest he become too real
yet without some moniker he is too uncontained
I cannot know him, this id? curse? devil?
ancestral apparition? projected back
to rail at me for what I've done
my bloody conscience.

Winds of Aeolus
Susan E. Rogers

"Miss, you ain't got nothin' else goin' out back, right? 'Cause that's the last time I'm goin' out there. Wind's blowing like a mother and it's too freakin' creepy. Like eyes watching me from everywhere." The moving guy's face was as white as the porcelain sink.

His partner called from the hall. "Hey, Al. I need help getting this mattress up them stairs."

Christine smiled and shrugged as Al stomped by her. She blew a puff of air upward that ruffled through her wispy bangs and bounced back at her eyelashes from the brim of her baseball cap. She hated moving. She vowed to herself, for the thousandth time, that this would be her last move. For—ever. Besides, she couldn't afford to go anywhere else.

This move was good for her, though, thanks to her mother who inherited the property from her eccentric uncle, an archeologist the family rarely saw between his digs in Greece and his teaching position at the small Florida college nearby. Mom tried renting it to other professors, but they never stayed more than one semester. When Christine got divorced, the house had been vacant for almost a year. She and her mother decided it would be the perfect place for Christine to make a fresh start and get back on her feet.

She picked up the box marked *Dishes* and brought it over to the counter near the sink. Her eyes strayed to the scene beyond the window. Everything was calm, no wind at all despite Al's complaint. It didn't look creepy to her, just... what was a good word... Neglected? Unkempt? That was it. Nothing a good cleanup and some fresh plantings wouldn't take care of. She gazed out over the area of the back yard she could see from the window. It was a good size for this part of town and gave her privacy from the neighbors on all three sides. The garden was one of the reasons she decided to live here, along with her divorce and the fact that it was free.

A flash of light reflected off the fountain into her eyes, mesmerizing her as she stared out the window.

"Miss? Miss? You all right?"

Al's voice broke into her trance.

"Uh... Yes. I'm uh... fine." She blinked a few times and held onto the counter for support.

"Everything's outa the truck." He held out a sheet of paper. "Here's the receipt. Wanna sign on the bottom there?"

"What?... Oh, sure," she said as she took the paper and pen he offered. "Sorry, my mind was somewhere else."

She wagged her head to clear it and signed the receipt. As she handed it back, her eyes glanced at the clock lying on the counter. It couldn't be four o'clock. She remembered the hands pointed at two-fifteen when she took it out of the box just before Al came in from out back. How did she lose almost two hours?

"You sure you're okay? 'Cause this place is weird, especially that back yard." He flipped his head toward the window.

"Everything's fine. Don't worry." She managed a half-smile. "Thanks a lot. You guys did a great job."

Al ripped off the top copy of the receipt and handed it to Christine. The rest he folded and stuck in his back pocket. "Okay. If you say so."

They shook hands and he turned to leave. Christine heard him mumble as he walked toward the front door.

"You couldn't give me a million bucks to stay here."

***

From the back door, Christine squinted into the bright cloudless sky. Stray blond curls escaped her ponytail and played around the corners of her dark brown eyes. She brushed them away absent-mindedly. A beautiful day to tackle the garden. She spent the past week unpacking boxes and getting settled into the house, around her work-from-home schedule. This was her first foray into the yard to survey the tangle of brush and weeds, and decide how she could tame the neglected wilderness.

A brick patio spread over the area at the bottom of

the stairs. A table and chairs were off to one side where Al the mover had set them next to the barbecue grill. Beyond the patio, the yard was laid out like the courtyard of an English country estate, brick walkways dividing the symmetrical geometric-shaped sections around a fountain in the center. She shaded her eyes with her hand and looked up.

The perimeter was defined by tall foxtail palms that offered shade and protection from the central Florida sun. The long fronds rustled like tissue paper as they swayed in the light breeze. Christine dropped her eyes to ground level where the scene wasn't quite as idyllic.

A ten foot square of brick, laid out in a herringbone pattern around the base of the tall three-tiered cement fountain, was the axis of the garden. A matching brick path extended in each compass direction from the center square, dividing the yard into quadrants. More bricks, placed end to end, outlined these derelict patches that used to be thriving flower beds, now filled with dead stalks and dried seed heads. The bricks must once have offered a smooth, even walkway around the yard, but now they tilted and slanted in all directions, looking more like a lopsided fun-house track.

Withered tangles of overgrown crab grass and creeping vines covered the soil. She expected to smell rotted vegetation, but there was nothing except warm air.

"This is definitely going to be a challenge," Christine muttered as she picked her way across the uneven bricks.

The surface of the six-foot cement fountain was a random mosaic of chipped paint and exposed concrete. Green stains ringed the inside of the wide bowls where stagnant water collected from the rain and then evaporated in the heat. She pushed back a strand of hair that blew into her eyes and looked up at a tarnished copper puffy-cloud head blowing curlicues of wind from its mouth, like an angel atop a Christmas tree. Except this topper didn't look so glorious with its puckered face and glowering cut-out eyes as it wobbled in the slight breeze.

"Hey, what's that?"

Beneath the finial, camouflaged by paint flakes and

greenish-blue patina, a perfectly preserved brass mask looked directly into her eyes. It was like nothing Christine had seen before. Wild waves of hair and a long curled beard, tossed by a forgotten wind, framed wide protruding eyes, bulging cheeks and a long, slender nose. The most prominent feature, however, was the mouth. Exaggerated, swollen lips were pursed around a circular hole in the metal, about the size of a quarter.

A jumbled wad of hardened fiberglass and rotting fabric were stuffed in the mouth hole, like somebody tried to do the job in a hurry. She grabbed a corner of the cloth and tugged, but it was fused tightly in place. A tiny swatch of threads ripped away and stuck to her finger, releasing a thin draft of air that puffed into her eye from one side of the hole. She blinked and shook her hand like it was on fire to get rid of the bits of fabric.

Grabbing the phone from her pocket, she took a few steps back and snapped a photo of the mask. When the picture came up on her screen, jagged flashes of light bounced back at her from the eyes. A shiver ran down her body.

"Heh... Just a trick of the light." She couldn't take her eyes off the mask on the fountain as she stepped backwards toward the porch. When her heel hit the bottom step, she turned and ran into the house, slamming the door behind her. She leaned against the counter, out of breath.

"Come on, I'm not going to be like Al." She got control of herself and looked out the window. Everything was fine. When she checked the picture again, the flashes were nothing more than sparkles of reflected sunlight. She shoved the phone in her pocket and flung open the door. "Okay. We're not going to waste this beautiful day. Let's do this."

Armed with spade, rake, and shovel, Christine dragged a trash barrel over to the garden bed in the northwest corner, avoiding a look at the mask as she passed. The breeze blew harder now and felt warmer. She wiped beads of sweat from her upper lip and tugged her baseball cap tighter down on her head, tucking up the loose strands of hair.

With hands on her hips, she surveyed the bed. About sixteen feet square, it was bordered on the two outer sides by a rusted black wrought iron fence that backed up to the trunks of the palms. Between the posts, elaborate scrolls and spirals mimicked those of the cloud finial's windy breath. She cringed at the ten inch fleur-de-lis shaped bayonet spikes that topped every other post.

"That'll keep the neighbors out."

A bead of blood oozed from her fingertip after she just barely touched the point of the closest one. She spied a small furry body impaled on one of the wicked blades near the corner and shuddered.

"I've got to get rid of these spikes." She sucked the blood from her finger. "The last thing I need is a kid in the neighborhood getting hurt on them." As much as she hated to deal with the dead mouse, there wasn't much choice. She put on her gloves and grabbed a plastic bag.

"Why would anybody put these on their fence, anyway? Sorry, little guy," she said to the mouse whose corpse crumbled to dust when she touched it with the spade, sprinkling the ground with shattered bones and tattered skin. She scooped up the pile and dumped it in the bag, holding it at arm's length until she tossed it in the trash.

She turned and surveyed the garden. Bushes were once planted around the perimeter inside the fence, but now they were clumps of dried up twigs. She attacked the first shrubby skeleton, stabbing the point of the shovel in the soil and pushing down on the handle. A cloud of powdery dirt exploded into the air and Christine breathed it in before she had a chance to react. The fine dust coated her throat and nostrils, making her sneeze and choke.

"Blech! Pthht" She dropped the shovel and turned away from the hole as she tried to spit out the dirt that covered her tongue. "Gross!" Something on the ground caught her eye. "What is that?"

She bent over the gray patch. It wasn't until she grabbed a stick and turned it over that she realized it was a dead squirrel. One beady eye looked up at her from what looked like a flat piece of leather with a few clumps of bristly fur still attached to the desiccated mummy.

"At least it doesn't smell." She picked it up with the stick and threw it in the barrel with the mouse, then went back to work.

The rest of the job didn't go so easily. Most of the shrubs seemed cemented in the dry, hard ground. It took two hours to dig out all the withered remains. When she got to the last bush, she found another dead animal, this time a crow. The flattened body lay on the ground between the last two shrubs. Piles of black feathers littered the ground and the tip of the beak was stuck in the dirt. She dumped it in the trash with the others. By then she was tired, sore, and shrouded with a coating of fine powdered soil. She pulled out the last bush and called it a day.

"Everything's so dried out. I might have to put in some irrigation," she mused as she walked back to the house.

The steamy water of the shower felt good on her overworked muscles as she scrubbed away the film of dirt and washed her hair. She was toweling dry when she realized that, except for the three mummified bodies, there had been no sign of life besides herself in the garden the whole time she was out there. No squirrels ran through the trees, no birds called, and no insects buzzed. She hadn't seen one beetle scuttling through the soil when she pulled out the bushes.

"That's weird..." The thought sent a shiver down her spine.

***

Light rain pattered against the window. Every muscle in her body groaned when Christine rolled over to get out of bed. Her throat was parched and dry and her cracked lips stung when she ran her tongue over them.

"Ow! How did this happen?" She smeared on lip balm before heading to the kitchen to make coffee. Nothing felt this sore when she went to bed last night.

The rain put a stop to continuing yesterday's work in the garden. She turned on the TV to catch the weather and scratched at an itchy spot on her arm. White marks raked across her skin and left tiny flakes in their wake.

"How did I get so dried out?" She slathered lotion all over her body, checking her dehydrated skin in the bathroom mirror.

The weather report forecast off and on light showers for most of the day. In the kitchen, she scooped grounds into the coffee maker and pressed the start button. She glanced out the window as she reached into the cupboard for a mug and froze. Wind tossed the palms from side to side and the rain came down in sheets across the back yard. It looked like a hurricane. Water overflowed the bowls of the fountain and sloshed onto the ground with the heavy gusts. She ran to look out the front window, but only sprinkles rippled the surface of the puddles.

That didn't make any sense. She headed back to the kitchen where the scene from the window was completely changed. Mist enveloped the garden and the water in the fountain sat undisturbed except for an occasional drip that broke the surface tension. Christine stared for several seconds.

"I don't get it. How could the storm break so fast?"

The mask on the fountain stared back at her. She flinched, sure she saw one corner of the mouth stretched up in a smirk. She yanked the curtains closed. It must have been an optical illusion caused by the mist. She was starting to sound more like Al.

After a quick breakfast and another layer of lotion, Christine downloaded the photo of the mask from her phone to her laptop and clicked on Google to search the image. In seconds, there were hundreds of pictures of brass masks. As she sorted through them, page by page from museums and antique sales catalogs, she began to see a pattern. Several of them were similar enough to the face on the fountain to identify it.

Aeolus, Greek God of the Winds. A vague memory from high school English popped into her head, something from Homer's Odyssey about Aeolus giving Odysseus a bag of wind to speed his journey home. The web page said Zeus made Aeolus the divine keeper of the winds, who could command them to rise or fall or shift however he chose. He kept the most violent storm winds locked away inside a cavern on his island, only releasing them upon order of one of the gods. Aeolus controlled their power and their potential to wreak havoc on the world.

Aeolus was now in her back yard, affixed to her fountain. Her uncle must have brought the mask back from an archaeological dig in Greece. She remembered her mother talking about all the artifacts in the house when they cleaned it out after he died. A museum in Boston bought most of the pieces. They must have overlooked the Aeolus mask.

A howling gust blew against the kitchen window, rattling the glass. She looked out at the fountain. The palms were motionless and the pooled water still. She shuddered and shut down her computer. Enough of gods and storms and wind. There were plenty of boxes left to unpack. She shivered again as she headed for the spare room.

***

Christine glanced at the clock. "The plumber should be here soon."

Yesterday, she noticed a small puddle on the utility room floor when she went to throw in a load of laundry. She thought rain came in through the window during the storm but she spotted a slow drip from a pipe that ran along the unfinished wall. She'd found a plumber who was available the next day, and asked the person in the office if he could check the pipes for the fountain while he was here to make the trip worth his while.

Half an hour later, Josh from ABC Plumbing knocked on the front door.

"Hi, come in. I'm Christine."

"Hi. Josh. You've got a fountain with a leak?"

"No." She giggled. "Two separate issues. The leak's in here and the fountain's in the back yard." She led the way to the utility room.

Josh took a quick look at the pipe. "This one's an easy fix." He pointed to the spot where a droplet was oozing its way out. "See? Your leak's right under that fitting."

He shut off the water main and went to work. Christine was about to leave him to it, but he started a conversation as he banged and twisted to remove the old coupling. She didn't mind. He was kind of cute with rumpled dark hair and a fluffy moustache. His bright blue eyes sparkled against his tan.

"So, did you just move in?" He worked at the pipe with a wrench. "I mean, I saw that stack over in the corner." He tilted his head in the direction of a pile of boxes. "Everything else looks pretty organized."

She smiled. "I moved in a week ago."

"Where're you from originally?" He gritted his teeth as he worked at the damaged pipe.

"Rhode Island."

"I thought I recognized that cute accent. I've got a friend from Barrington."

She felt the warmth rise in her cheeks. "I'm from East Providence, the next town over."

"Been there. Nice place." He glanced over at her. "So have you been to any of the Gulf beaches yet? I'd put ours up against the Rhode Island sand any day."

She laughed "No, I haven't had time yet. But I'll make sure I get there soon and make the comparison."

He grunted and a piece of metal fell to the floor with a clatter. "Well, maybe I can help you out with that." He wiped his sweaty palms on his pants and flashed her a toothy grin.

She'd avoided dating since her divorce, but the flirtatious undertone of their chitchat was fun. Maybe now would be a good time to start. "That might be nice." She offered a smile of her own.

He pushed on the new fitting and snapped it in place. "All set. You want to show me that fountain?"

Christine led him through the house and out the back door. A fresh breeze picked up as they walked over the brick path, rustling the palms above them.

"You've got your work cut out for you back here," Josh said as he looked around the yard. A blast of air grabbed at his cap but he caught it and yanked it down tighter.

"I know. Everything's completely dead." She wiped sweat from her forehead as she glanced over the yard. "But it does give me a blank slate. I can turn it into whatever I want."

"Bet it'll look great when you're done." He put his toolbox down in front of the fountain and wiped the back of his neck with a rag. "Pretty warm out here." He shoved the rag in his back pocket. "Well, let me check out this old baby and see what's up."

A gust skimmed across the surface of the rainwater in the lower bowl and sprayed him, soaking his shirt and the front of his trousers.

"Oh, no. I'll get a towel."

"Don't worry." He laughed as he shook the water from his hands and wiped drips from his face. "It's hot enough I'll be dry in a few minutes."

She shook her head. "I'll be right back."

Christine trotted toward the house. The breeze strengthened and nudged her along. When she reached the porch, she looked back at Josh, who stood facing the fountain with a hammer and chisel in his hands. He was tall and lean, and the rolled up sleeves of his blue work shirt emphasized the muscles in his arms. She blushed at her thoughts.

She was still daydreaming when she reached into the linen closet for a towel, but her reverie was abruptly interrupted by a chilling howl and a crash that echoed from outside. Her heart fluttered inside her rib cage as she leaned up over the counter and squinted. Josh wasn't there. She ran to the front door and threw it open. The ABC Plumbing van was parked in the driveway, but Josh wasn't in the driver's seat. She leaped down the steps two at a time and hurried to the other side. The doors were locked.

"Josh? Josh!"

There was no answer to her calls. As she walked toward the porch, she realized the wind had died down. She looked around the sides of the house to the eight foot stockade fence that separated the front yard from the back but didn't see Josh anywhere. Her eyes grew wide when she saw the palms thrashing beyond the fence over the garden. She shuddered and ran back inside.

"Josh? Josh? Are you in here?"

The house was quiet except for the whooshing of wind from out back. She looked through the kitchen window again. Aeolus glared at her across the yard, paralyzing her so she couldn't look away. Something was different about the face but she couldn't figure out what it was even as its gaze held her immobilized. A twig flew against the window and she jumped, the spell broken. She headed out the back door to look for Josh.

Outside, the scene was chaos. A fierce burning wind howled through the yard, uprooting dead stalks and roots. Dried leaves and deadfall zipped through the air, animated in a macabre dance by the gale. Christine grabbed the porch railing to keep from being blown off her feet. Her hair pulled loose from its ponytail and whipped around her sweaty face, into her eyes and mouth. Every breath was an effort as the wind sucked at her lungs and she gulped hot air.

"Josh!" She kept a tight grip on the rail and eased down the two steps to the ground as she croaked out his name. "Josh!" Her voice was lost to the roar of the wind.

She tried to look around the yard, but with her hair sticking to her face and debris flying everywhere, she couldn't focus. Once she let go of the railing, she concentrated all her effort on keeping her balance and staying upright. She bent forward, head down, with one arm out in front to steady herself and ward off the deadwood that aimed for her head as she watched her feet and fought her way to the fountain.

The wind drove against her, pushing her from one side to the other. When she got there, she grabbed onto the rim of the bottom bowl with a claw-like grip to keep from being blown over. Once she felt secure, she scanned the yard, turning her head away from the direction of the wind. She took one step at a time and circled the fountain, sliding her fists along the rough edge of the rim so she wouldn't let go.

She was half-way around when she spotted him. A

shrieking scream bubbled up from deep within her core. Josh hung head first over the wrought iron fence with two bayonet spikes protruding from his back below his shoulder blades. She ripped her hands from the fountain and dashed across the walkway toward him, shielding her eyes with her arm from the careening leaves and debris. Suddenly, her legs flew out from under her as she tripped over something solid and heavy. Her cries were cut off by the wind when she landed face down, sprawled across the hot bricks.

It took a few seconds to catch her breath. She rolled over onto her back with a groan and struggled to sit up. Josh's metal tool box was upside down at her feet, his tools scattered across the walkway. Her right knee oozed where layers of skin were scraped away. As she tried to get up, a branch flew into the side of her head. She whimpered and fell back on the bricks in a daze. When she pushed herself up again, her eyes fell on the mask and she froze.

The mouth was wide open. Engorged lips blew fierce wind into the air. Preoccupied with searching for Josh, she hadn't noticed the bits of fabric bobbing across the surface of the water or the chunks of fiberglass resin littering the bottom of the bowl. The hammer and chisel were on the ground beneath the fountain. Josh must have opened up the mouth hole and released the fury of the god.

She whimpered and limped backwards, never taking her eyes off Aeolus, until she stumbled over the brick border of the garden bed. With her arms outstretched, she struggled to keep her balance against the wind that shoved from one side and then the other as the cloud finial spun to change the direction of the onslaught. She turned and staggered across the uneven bricks.

Her momentum propelled her into Josh's body. She screamed as she fell against his thigh and pushed herself off, slipping in the dark pool that spread below him on the ground and landing on her back. Blood dripped from his mouth and chest and collected on the dry hard-packed soil. She scrabbled to get up from the sticky puddle. The hot coppery smell stuck in her nose and throat. There was no question he was dead.

The gale blew fiercer and hotter, scorching her already windburned skin, mottled with streaks of Josh's blood. She felt firm blisters on her parched lips when she ran her tongue over them to try and soothe them. The smell of cooked flesh from Josh's body made her gag. Gaping wounds oozed on his arms where the roasted skin split open and sloughed off, leaving muscle and fat exposed to the extreme heat. His thick hair was dried to clumps of straw.

Christine sniffled and reached under his chin to lift his head. The sniffles escalated to a stuttered whine when she saw his face. His mouth and eyes were wide open, the sockets empty, and the eyeballs withered to marbles dangling on his cheeks by withered strings of still-attached muscle. His shriveled tongue hung from the side of his mouth like a worn leather strap. She jerked her fingers away and the head flopped forward. Her whines broke down into gasping sobs and she sank to the ground, oblivious of the blood pooled around her, her cowering body hunched into a tight ball, face hidden between her knees. Her skin blistered under the pummeling of hot, arid wind, draining the moisture from her body.

A twig whacked against her shoulder. Her tangled hair blew wildly around her face as she turned toward the fountain. From where she sat in the bloody puddle, she could only see the edge of the mask, but the cloud finial continued to send scalding currents of air at her. She doubled over, wrapping her arms around her abdomen, as knots cramped inside her. The sneering cloud face stretched in maniacal laughter. Her eyes narrowed and squinted as she looked up at the bouncing finial, aimed at her and Josh. Her line of vision dropped to the glistening sunlight reflected from the brass mask of Aeolus, piercing her eyes and blinding her.

The knots morphed into cold steel in the pit of her stomach and thrust a bubble of bilious acid up to her throat. A roar burst through her swollen lips. She pushed herself up from the ground with clenched fists and fought to stay upright while being assaulted by each wave of blustery air. Bent over almost in half, she marched forward into the wind with determined steps. A short, thick branch scuttled along the ground and hit her ankle. She picked it up and brandished it in front of her as she trudged forward along the brick path.

Finally, she faced the fountain and the mask. The cloud head spun toward her and a new onslaught of broiling air shot from Aeolus's pursed lips. Her skin was on fire and sweat seeped from every pore, but her nerve endings were beyond sensing pain. She spied the hammer and chisel where Josh dropped them and her instinct took over. She took one step forward and picked up the hammer. Two more steps and she reached the fountain.

"Not going to let you drive me out." The words seethed from her clenched teeth. Raspy breaths punctuated each phrase. "MY home. My last stop. No where else. Not leaving."

Without hesitation, she planted one foot on the edge of the bottom bowl and hoisted herself over the top with one hand, still holding tight to the branch with the hammer in the other. The water was gone but the curved surface inside was slick with sludge left behind by the rain and she crouched to keep her balance. She reached up and grabbed hold of the edge of the second bowl and pulled herself to standing, her every breath released in a panting grunt. Scuds of torrid air slammed into her as she positioned her torso against the edge of the bowl to steady herself. Her eyes were slits against the wind but she saw Aeolus glaring at her.

Christine transferred the branch to her free hand and pulled her arm back. With a savage shriek, she plunged the branch into the mask's mouth hole, then used all her strength to swing the hammer against the end, wedging the piece of wood in the opening. Immediately, the wind was reduced to a weak trickle from the gaps around the edges where the branch didn't fit close. She pounded the branch again and again, until her arm couldn't lift the hammer one more time.

Her shoulders drooped, her strength depleted. She whimpered as she slid down from the fountain's bowl and slumped to the ground, exhausted and spent. The air was still and a cloud floated overhead, casting a brief respite of shade on her burnt skin. She lowered her head to her chin and a cry erupted from deep within her, followed by another and another, until her body quaked with silent racking sobs. She had no tears. Her body didn't have enough moisture left to squeeze out even one.

A faint noise creaked its way into her consciousness. She sucked in a final sob and listened to the sound of rubbing, twisting. Suddenly she knew. She jumped up in time to hear the pop as the branch flew out of Aeolus's mouth and shot through the air. The cloud face spun around and aimed its jeering grin directly at her as blasts of scalding wind from the mask assaulted her ravaged body.

Christine screamed, the piercing wail echoing around the yard. The wind continued to assail her as she climbed. She slipped in the sludge but didn't stop until she was propped against the middle bowl. She panted open-mouthed as she glared at Aeolus, her dried-out eyes narrowed in the wind. Her tongue was scorched and her lips raw from layers of skin peeled away. The eyes of the mask mocked her while the mouth blew searing gusts at her face. She raised the hammer and pulled back her arm, tense as a bowstring. Letting loose a howl overflowing with every bit of her rage and desperation, she slammed the hammer into the glinting brass face.

The first hit clipped the tip of the nose, crushing it to a concave pit. She drew back again and, with another wail of fury, drove the hammer's head through an eye socket. The wind exploded around her in a furious skirmish, squalls bashing against her, hurling any piece of loose debris in her face and against her arms. She latched onto the rim of the bowl with her free hand, her white-knuckled grasp daring the gale to yank her loose. Her frenzied blows continued, drawing strength from her innate will to survive. Each smash of the hammer on brass dented and defaced the mask, each pounding strike weakened the god's power.

Finally, with her strength used up and the hammer blows dwindled to rhythmic taps, Christine collapsed into the bowl of the fountain. The air was calm around her with a coolness that caressed her burnt skin as she lay on her side in the muck. Her shallow breathing calmed as she raised her head and looked up.

The brass face was battered, features no longer recognizable. The eyes were jagged gashes across the mangled brass. The mouth hole was hammered shut so not a puff of air could escape. She must have hit the finial at some point as the cloud dangled upside down from a bent-in-half post. Christine felt a single hot tear run down her cheek and saw the bloody drop hit her t-shirt. The hammer fell from her fingers as she covered her face with her hands.

She didn't know how long she stayed there. The sun was low in the western sky when she moved her hands and peeked out from swollen eyes. Her entire body was shrouded in a cocoon of pain. Dark red-purple skin on her arms and legs peeled in sheets to the raw and sensitive layers beneath. Her baby toes looked black and shriveled.

Josh's body still hung where she left it, the muscular shape collapsed and his flesh draped limply over its skeletal frame. The ground around him, and in every quadrant of the garden, was naked, blown bare of every dead and withered plant, an occasional branch tossed asunder as a reminder of the battle with the god.

She climbed slowly and awkwardly out of the fountain. Her legs felt heavy as granite posts, but she managed to shuffle to the back porch, up the two steps, and into the house. She stood in the middle of the kitchen, not sure what to do next. Her brain couldn't process any of this. She only knew the ordeal was over and she survived it, barely. Her whole body trembled but she felt nothing, physically or emotionally.

The car keys and her purse were on the table. She picked them up on her way to the front door. It slammed behind her as she left the house that was supposed to be her forever home, the place that was to offer her a fresh start on the next chapter of her life.

She backed out of the driveway and drove in the direction of town, toward the police station. The house grew smaller in the rear view mirror when she glanced up every few seconds until at last she turned the corner and it was lost from her line of sight. There was a hotel in town where she could stay for a few days until everything was sorted.

She sighed. "Somehow I have to make the police believe me." She looked in the mirror at her blistered and bloody face. "Maybe they will." She turned on the radio and the sounds of soft jazz filled the car, but even the music couldn't soothe her battered body and distressed soul.

***

In the back yard of the house, stillness flooded the air with the silence of death. High clouds passed overhead, skimming the yard with shade. An earthy smell infused the space, the odor of freshly turned dirt mixed with rot and decay. Josh's withered mummy dangled from the fence.

Suddenly, a faint noise echoed through the stillness. *ping!* Then a barely audible *creeeaaaak!*. Again silence for many minutes before a muffled *tap!tap!tap!* plinked like a bell wrapped in cotton. The sounds continued, not quickly, not rhythmically, just random counterpoints to the quiet. *creeeaaaak! ping! tap!tap!*

As dusk drew the light from the garden, a lone fly buzzed across the barren landscape. The insect zigged around Josh's dehydrated body, searching for sustenance. Not finding it's meal there, it zagged toward the fountain, hovered over the dried fleshy detritus that Christine left behind, then flew up toward the smashed piece of metal affixed to the post. In less than a second, the fly dropped to the bricks, all moisture sucked from its tiny body, leaving behind a dried out shell. A tiny spot in the center of the mutilated brass *popped!* and came to a point, looking like nothing so much as the tip of a nose.

Tylwyth Teg
Christian Dickinson

The country maid, at twilight, drove her kine
Beyond the bounds of farmland and of glade
When underneath the forest elm trees' shade,
She saw a crowd diminutive and fine.

In silken greens enrobed light as the air,
With eyes of blue and hair of golden-white.
They danced in rings and gamboled in delight
With feet unshod, and blooms upon their hair.

The tallest one come's to the maiden's knees:
"Oh lovely dear, come join us in our round.
We'll feed thee with the dew-drops from the rose
And let thy head with garlands sweet be crowned."
Led by the band, the maid most willing goes...
And leaves her kine to famish on the lees.

Them Boogers Will Get Y'all
Ginger Strivelli

My Mamaw had warned us young'uns. She always told us to watch out for haints and boogers.

Haints are just spirits though and can't do naught but scare the mess outta ya. Boogers are flesh and blood. They be some kind of flesh and blood. Some boogers might be humans, just deranged and evil ones. Some are creatures of some sort. Maybe the big river monsters them Cherokee told tales about or the bigfoots the tourists go galavanting about the woods looking for. Mamaw said them haints will stay away long as ya paint your doors and window frames in haint blue, which is a right pretty shade of blue, anyway. She had no advice on keeping the boogers away, she always just said not to go where they were, which was in the woods, swamps, and caves.

"Them boogers will get y'all," Mamaw had told me and all my cousins umpteen times.

Now, I didn't always listen to Mamaw. I skunk some of her moonshine and rock candy flu potion even when I didn't have nary a cough. I forgot to let the lightning bugs outta the mason jars at sunrise a few times when I caught a bunch so the wishes I had whispered to them the night before didn't come true those times. I even forgot to throw a pinch of cake or bread out to the fairy folk when I was a-cooking sometimes but the little fairies had never troubled me none.

Boogers will get y'all, though, as she said. I know that well enough now to follow my Mamaw's advice. I know because they 'bout got me once. I was a damn fool and decided to go into a cave I found when I was out picking blackberries in the woods. Now it was daylight and I wasn't too far out in them woods. So I was behaving responsibly till I found that cave.

I reckon I just let my imagination carry me away and got to thinking there might be some treasure in there. I put down my berry basket and just barely peeked in. It was dark as soot. I had my cell phone though and turned the flashlight on and marched in bold as brass. I should have backed out as soon as I saw them cave drawings though. Some looked like modern graffiti but others looked older than the hills. I kept on going even though the drawings all seemed to be warnings to go back.

The darkness wasn't too bad long as my cell phone flashlight worked which was about five minutes flat. Then it went out even though that battery had been at near full charge. In the darkness after that, I tried to spin around looking for the daylight from the cave entrance. I'd made too many dang turns and didn't see a hint of light coming from any direction.

"Hey, is anyone there?" I called out for some idiot reason. I knew I was all alone.

"Yes, Ma'am, young lady I am right c'here." A sickeningly sweet voice echoed through the inky black cave clear as a bell.

Well I jumped and hollered for it to go away as I ran around trying frantically to find my way back out into the sunshine. That is till I ran into the cave wall where them cave paintings were. I hit my noggin so hard I was seeing stars even in the dark. I actually was seeing stars, 'cause I saw them cave paintings on the wall dripping with my blood for a second before I was engulfed in the cave's cursed darkness again.

"I ain't scared of you." I lied. "I've heard tell of many a haint, they don't ever do nothing but howl."

It howled then laughed. "I'm no haint, child. No ma'am."

Damn it, I thought to myself. I was scared of it even if it had been just a haint but I was terrified if it was a booger. I started carefully backing up, trying to remember which way the cave entrance was from the cave art.

"You going the wrong way. You cain't get out the way ya came in. This here be a magic cave child...a black magic cave." The booger whispered and giggled.

"Black magic ain't real. Besides I know plenty of magic from my mamaw. She's a water witch, she'd banish you right back to whatever dimension you be from." I lied again, Mamaw hadn't taught me many of her spells or potions yet, I was only thirteen.

The booger laughed hysterically again. I could hear my heart beating in my ears. I was panting for breath in my panic. I tried to calm both my heart and lungs so as the booger didn't hear my fear.

"I can smell your fear, child. I don't need to hear it. I don't need to see either, this darkness don't hinder me one dang bit. You, though need the light, don't ya. The darkness seems to suck all your courage right outta ya, don't it?"

I was scared half to death by the thing being able to read my mind. I tried to not think about anything. I didn't know how to calm the smell of my fear, but I tried nonetheless. I tried to not let the darkness suck any courage out but I was pretty sure I didn't have any no ways. I reached out feeling for the nearest wall and when I found it I started feeling my way along it trying to find an opening in the tunnel of the cave I was lost in.

I yelped like a whipped dog when suddenly my hand on the wall came in contact with a cold furry hand. The Booger's other hand, well one of its others, it could have had a dozen for all I knew, but one grabbed my throat. It was just as furry and cold as the one I'd brushed against. I started thrashing about like a rainbow trout caught on a hook. I directly somehow managed to get my neck outta the booger's hand. I ran and ran and ran. Till I hit another one of the cave's rock walls. Smash! My head was bleeding a good bit from two wounds then.

"Your blood smells delicious, come hither, let me lick it."

"Booger, you ain't getting me. Go away, go on git!" I got a brief look at the booger when the stars before my eyes lit the cave for a moment when I banged my head again. It was eight foot tall, not wearing a stitch but covered with matted black fur. I might have thought it was a bigfoot or a bear, had the thing not been taunting me in plain English.

Soon as the stars faded into the darkness again I took off away from where I'd seen the booger lurking. I'd not seen its face but I was imagining that it had shark teeth or snake fangs or both. I knew a bit of Tsalagi, the Cherokee language that Mamaw had taught me. I thought maybe the booger would think I was casting a powerful banishing spell on it if I started babbling in that ancient language.

"Osiyo, agasga wesa!" I tried to sound magical and dangerous.

"Hello to you too child. I'm no cat…and it ain't a-raining in here in the dark. It might be raining outside, you won't get out to find out though." The booger said and laughed again.

"My Mamaw has fought off plenty of boogers in her time. I will fight you off."

"She ain't here child, no ma'am. She be way too wise to come in here like you did, I bet ya."

The booger was right, Mamaw always said the boogers will get y'all iffin' y'all go into a cave, swamp, or the woods at night. I was beating myself up for not listening when the thing snatched me up again by my throat. The thought I was 'bout to die ran through my head. I called out for help knowing dang well no one was there to hear.

Nevertheless, someone heard. Now I never really believed Mamaw about them fairies and how tossing out them a pinch of everything ya baked made them your friends before I saw those three appear glowing in the darkness. They were wee little things barely big as hummingbirds but they flew just as fast. They made a sound more like screeching brakes on an old car than the humming of hummingbirds. They flew right at the booger's face. That is when I got a look at it. It sure wasn't one of those demented human boogers. I didn't know what it was with its yellar eyes and big whiskered snout but I could tell it wasn;t any kind of human.

The booger screamed a line of cursing like you'd not hear in the worst old redneck bar at the fairies. Its real voice wasn't the sing-songy honey tongued voice it'd been teasing me in either; it sounded as scary as it looked.

One them fairies had shoved a tiny walking stick right into one of the booger's yellar eyes which made it drop me. I fell in a heap at its stinking feet. The three tiny winged fairies somehow were able to drag me to my feet. One of them pulled my left pigtail hard to make me look up. I could see some daylight up a narrow shaft in the cave ceiling. I went to climbing directly.

"No!" The booger roared. "You will not escape." It was still using its real hoarse voice instead of the sweet whisper.

I had my head and both arms outta the cave inside a briar bush, trying to crawl out when the booger got a-hold of both my legs and jerked me back in. I was kicking and screaming and crying. I just knew I was 'bout expire right then and there.

Suddenly Mamaw came running. She had come looking for me in the woods. I could see her coming at me through the trees as I got yanked back into the cave.

"Hang on!" She called. Two fairies were pulling her along by the lace collar of her housecoat. She was running fast as a stout old lady in pink fuzzy slippers could run in them rocky woods.

She had a mason jar with her, like the ones she kept her flu potion, ear ache potion, and such in. It was one I'd never seen before though and looked like it held only dirt. She got to the hole and reached down into it to grab a hold of my left arm. She told me to open the jar for her.

Now, I did as I was told. She threw the contents of the jar down the hole as she and the booger played tug of war with my shaking body.

The fairies were pulling me too though and the stuff she'd dumped on the booger seemed to be burning it as it was hollerin' in pain. The booger finally let go of my legs and Mamaw and the fairies fetched me right up outta that hole. We took to running even though we both knew that thing couldn't come out into the sunlight.

"What was in that jar, dirt?" I said through blood and tears running down my face.

"Graveyard dirt, salt, and vinegar." Mamaw said panting as she 'bout tripped on a rotting tree stump. "Iffin' the fairies hadn't come got me, you'd be dead, girl."

"They helped me too. I didn't think fairies were real." I

said, finally able to breathe normally again.

"You didn't think boogers were real either now did ya?" Mamaw used her gown tail to wipe the blood and tears from my face.

"No, ma'am but I sure know now." I said then promised mamaw I'd teach my own grandkids about the boogers when I was old and wise like her.

The Girl Who Fed On Nightmares.
A.A. Alhaji

i saw an owl
cried twice before dawn
with the night as an alibi
i see mortals in mourning clothes
my mother sets her dreamcatcher,
she collects all my nightmares
in one basket & eats them overnight.
i see my brother in the moon orbs
he lives on through cycle of rebirths
i carry his soul in my mouth, a reincarnated cherry from a
      random pick of autumn, a dead end to the matyrs
      who lived till through dying breaths, re-writing fate
      with pens made from branches
of a tree that weighs our sins.

Thanks for the Memories
Mike Murphy

Kenneth live-parked the limousine in front of the soup kitchen. Dryer, in the seat behind him, looked out through the tinted window. The extreme heat of the day was rising in the air like waves. The men in line looked shabby and dirty – people he would *never* associate with if his need wasn't so vital.

"Here we are, sir," the hulking, uniformed chauffeur said.

"Very good, Kenneth," Dryer answered.

"Need I remind you, Mr. Dryer," Kenneth continued, "that this is *not* the best area of town?"

"No," his boss answered him, "you don't have to remind me." He looked at the men in line again and wondered if he could *really* do this. "If you consider it," he went on, "what better place to find someone who needs the money and might agree to my proposal."

"Logical, sir. As always."

"Sad, isn't it?" Dryer continued after a sigh.

"Sir?"

"Such poverty."

His chauffeur paused and said, "You're *certain* you want to go through with this?"

"Absolutely."

"Even with the possible repercussions?" Kenneth asked.

"Yes." Dryer pinched the bridge of his nose and took a deep breath of the air conditioning. "I've thought about this long and hard," he told Kenneth.

"If you say so, sir," Kenneth answered.

"You understand my instructions?"

"Yes."

"You are *not* to enter the library until I call you or until dawn, whichever comes first."

"I understand," Kenneth confirmed. "This could be *very* dangerous."

Dryer replied, "I understand that. I don't think

anyone knows the possible danger of this more than I. Your concern is appreciated."

"You've always been very good to me, sir," Kenneth spoke through the lump forming in his throat, "and I consider you a friend."

"You're talking as though we'll never see each other again!"

"Neither of us knows what might happen."

"Must we assume the worst?" Dryer asked.

There was a long, uneasy pause. "Now, sir?" Kenneth asked.

"Yes," his employer answered from behind him. "Now."

Kenneth turned off the ignition. The lack of air conditioning immediately became apparent. Both men began to sweat, partly from the heat of the day and the rest from fear. The chauffeur lumbered out of the driver's-side door and swung it closed behind him. Then, with some fanfare, he opened the passenger door to allow his employer to exit. Dryer instantly felt many eyes upon him. "We certainly are attracting a lot of attention, aren't we?" he observed.

Kenneth chuckled under his breath and offered, "I suppose it's not every day that you see a limousine parked outside of a soup kitchen."

Like a coach about to deliver a pep talk, Dryer approached the men waiting in line. Kenneth followed behind him, ready to pounce at the merest threat. "Is there anyone here who is 43 years old?" Dryer called out. The men in the queue looked at him oddly. "43?" Dryer continued. "I have a business proposition for anyone who is *43* years old."

As the men began to mumble among themselves, one stepped forward. He was shorter than Dryer and was sporting several days' growth of beard. His clothes were dirty and ill fitting. "What are you doing here, mister?" he asked.

Dryer felt Kenneth stir behind him. "Not to worry," he said. He faced his new acquaintance. "As I mentioned," he continued, "I have a business proposition."

"What kind of proposition?"

"A proposition where the other person needs to be 43 years old."

"I'm 43," the man replied. "What's it to ya?"

Dryer smiled an ear-to-ear smile. "So *good* to meet you!" he said. "Allow me to introduce myself: William P. Dryer." He thought briefly of holding out his hand for the man to shake, but then reconsidered it.

A bell rang in the man's brain. "I've read about someone with that name," he said.

"It was probably me," Dryer replied with mock humility.

"You're a millionaire, right?"

"*Many* times over, Mr. . ."

"Denver," the man replied. "Jack Denver."

"Pleased to meet you."

Denver stole some appreciative glances at the limo. "That's a nice car you've got there."

"It's one of my favorites," Dryer went on.

"You have *more* than one limo?"

"I do." Dryer continued, "Now, about my business proposition."

"Uh huh."

"You said you're 43 years old?"

"I did, and I am."

"Wonderful! So am I."

"Great!" a confused Denver replied with fake enthusiasm. "What's the deal?"

"I think it would be better to talk about it at my home," Dryer suggested. "Kenneth will drive us." On cue, the chauffeur opened the passenger door for the gentlemen. Dryer could see that his new friend was apprehensive. "Is there a problem, Jack?" he inquired. "May I call you 'Jack?'"

"Sure you can."

"Is there a problem?" Dryer asked again.

"It's just. . . just that I was waiting for lunch, and I'm pretty hungry."

"Oh, I see," Dryer responded. "What would your repast consist of in that establishment?"

"Huh?"

"What's for lunch?" Dryer asked in more common words.

Denver paused to recall. "I *think* today," he answered, "it's chicken sandwiches, coleslaw, fries, and coffee."

"Jack," Dryer continued, draping one arm over Denver's shoulders, "if you come to my home to *consider* my offer, my chef will prepare a *much* better lunch for you."

"Like what?" Denver inquired eagerly.

"How about a thick steak – cooked to your specifications, of course – with fresh vegetables, potato, a fine dessert, and a wonderful wine?"

"All that for *considering* your offer?" Denver asked.

"Yes."

"What if I hear your offer and say 'no?'"

"I'll have Kenneth drive you anywhere in the city you'd like," Dryer answered. "You will have lost nothing and gained a wonderful meal."

Denver was unsure. "I don't know," he said.

"If you'd like," Dryer added, "I can have Kenneth wait in line for you while you decide in the comfort of my air-conditioned limousine."

Though the thought of Dryer's bodyguard waiting in line did amuse Denver, he paused briefly and said, "No, that's OK. I'd. . . I'd like to go with you."

#

The walls of the oak-paneled library were covered with books. Denver had no doubt they were all first editions. From their conversation over lunch, he knew that Mr. William P. Dryer would accept nothing less. The framed art, he also knew, were originals. No cheap prints here. "Did you enjoy your meal?" Dryer asked.

"Oh, yeah," Jack answered his host. "It was the best I've had in a *long* time."

"Randolph is an excellent chef." He pointed at the two leather wing-back chairs that sat facing each other in the middle of the room. "Please have a seat," he said.

Denver sat, amazed at the luxuriousness. "I feel like

I'm *melting* into this chair!" he said.

"Italian leather – very comfortable." Dryer paused briefly to gesture about the room. "I like to surround myself with the best," he said. "May we discuss the proposition now?"

"Sure thing."

"Please remember that you are free to decline at any time with no hard feelings."

"I know," Denver responded. "What's the deal?"

"I want to buy something of yours."

"With all those cars, with this house, with servants," Denver said, amazed, "there's something of *mine* that you want to buy? *What*?"

His host paused and then matter-of-factly answered, "Your memories."

"Come again?"

"Your *memories*," Dryer reiterated. "I want to buy them from you."

"My. . . memories? How. . ."

"I assure you that I can do it."

Denver chuckled and asked, "What's the going price for memories nowadays?"

"I'm prepared to offer you $10,000."

"*Ten thousand?*"

"In cash," Dryer added.

"You're puttin' me on," Denver said dismissively.

"I'm serious."

"Alright," Denver continued, "just to play devil's advocate, let's say you're being straight with me. How long have you been able to do this memory-buying thing?"

"For many years," Dryer answered his guest. "I think it all started on the night I killed my father."

"You killed. . ." Denver began, shocked.

"I did," Dryer went on proudly. "Does that surprise you?"

"Well, *yeah*."

"He was a *dreadful* man," Dryer explained, "always beating my dear mother and me." He looked at his guest. "You seem uncomfortable," he said.

"I *sure* am."

"Would you like to leave?" Dryer asked him. "I could ring Kenneth."

"I. . . uhm. . ."

"Of course, you haven't heard me out, and you *would* be passing up your chance at the $10,000."

Denver paused briefly, the thought of all that cash going down the drain played across his mind. "You're right," he finally said. "That wouldn't be fair. I should hear the money. . . uh, hear *you* out."

"I assure you I have no hostile intent. You're perfectly safe."

"I believe you," Denver responded, clearing his throat. "You were mentioning," he went on, "k-killing your. . . father."

***

Mr. Dryer drank too much, and when he drank, he got violent – usually, though not always, towards his wife. Bill remembered many nights as a young boy where he pulled the blankets over his head and wished for it all to stop.

***

Bill, then a sophomore in high school, heard the music before he entered the small apartment the three of them shared. Big bands. That meant only one thing: His father was drunk again. Oftentimes, when he was drunk, his father would draw a steaming-hot bath, put the little radio they kept on the windowsill on a chair beside the tub – his hearing wasn't the best – and climb into the water. Very often, he would fall asleep in there.

Bill peeked in through the cracked door. There he was – *almost* asleep. The smoke from his cigarette mingled with the steam coming off of the water, which was fogging up the vanity mirror.

Never a violent person, Bill was surprised at the naked rage building inside of him. All those years of abuse to his dear mother and him pushed him over the edge. He seized his chance! His father never even saw him. He swung the door open wide, jumped into the bathroom, and kicked the radio off the chair and into the tub.

The electricity from the radio crackled and danced

over the water. The naked man bucked wildly, as though a crazy puppeteer was pulling all of his strings randomly.

I've done it! Bill thought. He and his mother would be free! No more abuse. Once their bruises faded, there would be nothing to remind either of them of this evil man. He smiled at the thought. As he turned to leave the bathroom, an arc of electricity leapt out of the tub and hit him behind the left ear, propelling him into the next room.

The next thing Bill remembered was starting to wake up on the couch, his mother hovering over him. She had been crying – her eyes were bright red – and her voice was wracked in sadness. "Bill, honey," she explained through tears, "the doctor says you'll be alright. You need your rest."

"Rest," Bill muttered, fading in and out from the world.

"I don't know if you can understand me right now," she went on. "There's been a terrible accident. Your father's dead."

"Dead?" her son replied weakly.

"You've been hurt, but you'll be fine," she continued, gently stroking his hair. "You sleep now."

Bill tried to look sad that his father was dead. He did a good job. No one suspected him. His mother told the authorities of her husband's propensity to drink, and his death was ruled accidental. His father was dead, and Bill was *happy*. He felt that Mother must be too. Whatever the future held, it would be better than what had been. They were rid of that awful man.

***

Not much later, Bill discovered that the electric shock had given him a power that would change his life.

***

"The ability to take other people's memories," Denver stated.

"Not *take*, Jack. I can't *take* them," Dryer explained. "The other person has to agree to the. . . transfer."

"The electricity did that?"

"I can see no other explanation." Dryer noticed that his guest was starting to fidget in his previously comfortable chair. "You seem uneasy again,"

"Well, *sure* I am. You just told me how you killed your dad!"

"*Father.*"

"Dad, father. What's the difference?" Denver said dismissively.

Dryer sat bolt upright in his chair. His face reddened, and he pointed an accusing finger at the man across from him. "There's a *big* difference," he said angrily. "A *dad* doesn't get drunk and beat you and your mother. A *dad* doesn't make you afraid to stay out late or fall asleep. A *dad* doesn't belittle you at every turn and say that he wishes you had never been born!" He rubbed his temples and tried to regain his composure. "There's a big difference, Jack," he stated, settling back in his chair. "A *big* difference."

"I'm. . . I'm sorry," Denver answered quickly.

Dryer felt the need to explain more. "Please forgive my outburst. I suppose that I'm more sensitive to the differences because of my past," he said. "Did you have a *dad*, Jack?"

"Oh yeah," Denver reminisced. "We went fishin' and huntin' together. We played a lot of ball. We laughed all the time. He was a funny guy."

"I envy you," Dryer replied. "He has passed on?"

"Around seven years ago."

"I am sorry."

Denver knew he needed to hear more of his host's story, though he was uncertain if he really wanted to. He was leaning towards refusing Dryer's request and getting the hell out of there. But 10 Gs! Where would he *ever* get that kind of money?

"You were saying," he went on, against his better judgment, "how you learned about your. . . power."

"One of the first instances I remember was in high school. . ."

***

It was the day of the big American history exam. Bill had forgotten all about it and hadn't studied one bit. If he *had* remembered, he might have chosen not to study anyway. He wasn't an honor roll kind of student.

The class know-it-all was Percival Caruthers, a weird kid. He had a face full of acne and wore *huge* glasses. As the lecture was coming to a close, Percival would remind the teacher that he hadn't given out homework yet. This was one of the reasons no one in class liked him. His voice was always squeaky. Puberty wouldn't give up on Percival.

He walked into the classroom, all full of himself. He had obviously studied *a lot.* He had the time since hardly anyone talked to him. His I'm-better-than-you-are attitude was very annoying. Unfortunately for Bill, because of the teacher's alphabetical seating plan, Percival sat right next to him.

"How long did you study, William?" Percival asked, settling into his desk.

"Not one minute," Bill replied.

"Oh dear!" Percival continued, genuinely concerned. "This test counts for forty percent of our grade."

"I know. I *know.*"

"If you flunk it, you'll end up in summer school," Percival reminded him. "What are you going to do?"

Bill leaned towards Percival. "Percy, old pal. . ." he began.

"No, William. I will *not* help you cheat," Percival replied adamantly.

"Why not? You have before."

"That's because I thought you were my friend."

"I'm *not* your friend?" Bill asked, feigning insult.

"You're my friend when you *need* me," Percival continued. "You think I never noticed that? I'm not dumb, you know."

"Come on, Percy!"

"No," Percival replied. "We'll get caught, and Mr. Bossio will give us *both* zeroes. My dad will be really upset if my grade point average dips."

"*Percy.*"

"No, William," he said, his voice getting even squeakier. "I refuse. Absolutely not!"

"You don't have to do anything special," Bill

continued. "Just write a little bigger than usual. I'll do the rest."

"No."

"I'll *pay* you. Five bucks?"

"I said 'no,'" Percival answered with finality. "I wish you had come to me sooner. We could have studied together."

"*That* would have been a blast."

"I'm sorry, William. I wish I could help you – I *really* do – but there's no time now."

Mr. Bossio walked through the classroom door as the bell rang. The test questions and blue books were passed back from row to row. The students, he announced, would have one hour to complete the test. Bill shot a last look at Percival, who moved his blue book closer to him.

At that moment, the now-familiar feeling came over Bill. He felt nauseous. His ears rang a little, and his vision went briefly blurry. When those symptoms eased, more than he *ever* wanted to know about American history flooded his brain: The Articles of Confederation, the Alien and Sedition Acts, the Emancipation Proclamation. Things that he had never *heard* of before were now swimming around his head begging to be put down on paper. He grabbed his pen and started writing furiously in the blue book, afraid that this sudden knowledge would dry up.

Out of the corner of his eye, he saw a very distressed-looking Percival Caruthers staring blankly at his blue book, writing nothing. He shot a questioning glance over at Bill, who hid his blue book with his left arm.

***

"I aced the test and brought my average way up," Dryer told his guest. "Mr. Bossio congratulated me on my grade, and Mother was thrilled."

"And Percival?" Denver asked.

"He got his first F," Dryer answered, amused.

"You think that you somehow got all this history knowledge from *him*?"

"I do. He wished that he could help me –

remember? – and I wanted American history knowledge. Two *willing* parties. It's the only conclusion."

***

"How long do these memories stay with you?"

"Forever."

"You don't forget *a thing?*" Denver queried, surprised.

"Oh, sometimes a newly purchased memory might overlap an older one. I *still* remember a great deal of what was on that test."

Denver looked about the ornate library. "And," he said, "you've used this ability to get rich."

"I *certainly* have," Dryer said proudly. "You'd be surprised at the trade secrets, for instance, that business people are willing to give up for greed. Once those secrets were mine, I used them and built on them. Slowly but surely, I amassed my fortune."

"Why do you want to buy *all* of my memories?"

"The power isn't perfect, Jack," Dryer explained. "Let's say, for instance, that I bought the memory of someone's extra-special tenth birthday party. When I receive that memory, it doesn't necessarily erase the memory of my *real* tenth birthday party. I can never know in advance where a new memory will lodge in my brain. Because of that, I now remember *three* tenth birthday parties, *eight* first loves, *six* college graduations. . . you get the idea. My mind is a jumble."

"What happens to the people you buy these memories from?" Denver asked.

"They're *fine*. They merely have that gap in their memory."

"But now you want to buy *all* of my memories."

"Yes, to erase everything else and give me *one* coherent life."

"But aren't you certain to lose the memories of your mother this way?" Denver asked.

"It is possible. . . even *probable*," Dryer said sadly. "It's a risk I have to take. I'm sure she would forgive me."

Jack asked the big question on his mind: "What will happen to *me* if I go through with this?"

Dryer paused and looked seriously at him. "I don't know," he said. "I've never purchased *all* of someone's memories. I *really* don't know."

***

This guy is *nuts,* Jack thought. There's no way he can do this! He *thinks* he can. All I have to do is humor him, and I get $10,000. *Ten grand.* What I could do with ten big ones! I just have to put on a little show. Once it's over, I can leave with the money and never see this weirdo again.

***

"Jack?" Dryer said, waiting for his guest's answer.

"If I say 'yes,'" Denver asked, "when do I get my money?"

Dryer pointed at a small end table beside his guest. "Open the top drawer," he said. Denver did as instructed, and his eyes lit up at the pile of green before him.

"Pick it up," Dryer urged him. "Look at it. *Touch* it." Denver withdrew the money from the drawer and fingered each individual bill. They felt good in his hands. "Imagine what you could do with it," Dryer continued. "No more waiting in line for chicken sandwiches."

"Certainly *not.*"

"Remember, Jack," Dryer went on, "you can turn me down if you like. All you have to do is put the money back in the drawer and shut it. I'll ring Kenneth, and you can go."

Denver paused for a moment. In his brain, there was a scrap going on between the reality of the money in his hands and the chance that maybe, just *maybe*, Dryer was being sincere.

"I've made up my mind," he said, the fight over.

"Yes?"

Jack reached out and closed the drawer, the money still in his hands. "What do I need to do?" he asked.

"Simply answer my question," Dryer responded, starting to smile. "Remember, once you agree, there's no turning back."

"I understand," Jack added, clutching the money tightly.

"Are you ready?"

"As I'll ever be," Jack replied with a sigh.

Dryer leaned forward in his chair, fixing his gaze on Denver. "Jack," he asked, "do you want to sell me *all* of your memories for $10,000?"

"Yes," Jack replied, sure he was in the company of a lunatic. "Yes, I do."

Those feelings came over Dryer once again, only magnified many-fold. The pain was *intense. Could this be right?* he wondered. Maybe the symptoms were worse because he was getting all-new memories? His head pounded, his nose began to gush blood, and his leg muscles started spasming.

Shocked, Denver leapt from his chair, the $10,000 – now meaningless to him – falling to the floor at his feet. He screamed a few times in agony, jamming his palms against his temples in an attempt to stop the fire in his brain. After a prolonged, vocal cord-shattering scream, his body went limp, and he fell back into the chair – dead.

Dryer sprang up. He tore at his eyes. "*Too much!*" he yelled, before also falling back into his chair.

***

Kenneth arrived at dawn, as he had promised he would. The two men were slumped in their chairs. Jack was dead, his jaw slack, staring through glassy bloodshot eyes at nothing in particular. His newfound riches lay scattered on the floor below him and on the seat cushion – just so many worthless green pieces of paper now.

Dryer had neglected one vital thing that became apparent when Kenneth found Denver's driver's license: While Jack *was* 43 years old, he was approximately six weeks *older* than Dryer.

The memories his employer purchased had overloaded his brain.

Dryer, his eyes also glassy and bloodshot, sat slumped in his chair, mumbling repeatedly in a child's voice of the only memories that remained in his damaged brain – those of his father.

"Daddy, no. Daddy, please *help*."

The Sacred Cats of Burma
Lavinia Kumar

When death is near
a cat may move your soul.

A white cat, the first, held the soul
of its dead high priest master.
It faced a south door,
became gold like the temple goddess,
turned its face, its tail, dark colors of earth,
drew into its eyes the sapphire sky.
Only its four paws
remained dazzle white.

And on the seventh day,
this cat died
bringing one hundred new white cats
to the temple,
for a new high priest to be chosen.

These cats carry souls,
trees must bear winter.
Time must move on.

The Man with Red Hands
A.K. McCarthy

Dead leaves were still clinging to the trees when Stephen Marquardt walked into the forest alone.

The 8-year-old boy was almost always alone. His mother had died giving birth to him, a sin for which Stephen had never forgiven himself. His father worked in the mine by day and could be found at the bottom of a glass at night.

He'd become friendly with a couple kids at the schoolhouse, but not the kind of friendship that extended beyond school hours.

So Stephen spent much of his time alone, or with the family goat, Bartleby. When Bartleby died — Stephen's father said it was of old age — Stephen felt a deep loneliness.

His chest and his stomach became one, a bottomless hollow pit in his torso. He'd feel it start to ache as the school day came to an end, and hot tears would rise through the pit and up to behind Stephen's eyes as he walked home from school. He'd go into the house, unable to get words past the lump in his throat, and fall onto his uncomfortable bed.

Before the goat's death, Stephen had at least been able to talk with him and find warmth in the animal's fur. Now, he had nobody.

Until the gifts started showing up.

They were bouquets of twigs and herbs, tied neatly together with roots. A steady, caring hand had curated them and bundled them together. They looked like they all came from different trees and plants. They had taken time to put together, and clearly came from the forest outside of town.

Stephen found them out back, in the center of a fenced-in patch of dirt where Bartleby had lived.

Stephen swiped a ribbon from a girl at school and picked a couple dying flowers on his way home. He tied the makeshift, morbid bouquet together and marched into the forest at the edge of town.

The small boy peered up at the leaves on the trees, which were burning brightly with their death colors. The small town lay in a valley in the mountains, and he found himself walking up a somewhat steep incline through the trees.

He walked until he found what he thought was a fitting place — a large boulder with a flat top. A small pool of rainwater had gathered in one spot atop the hulking stone. Stephen placed his bouquet near it, reaching as far as his small limbs would let him.

He stepped back and admired his work. A cool autumn breeze swept through the woods, and he looked up and saw the trees swaying above him. Suddenly cold, Stephen turned and marched toward town. He didn't stay to see if his new friend would show up.

***

The next day, Stephen's chest finally felt full as he headed home from school. No tears came. No lump formed. He ran to the backyard and his heart leapt when he saw another bundle of sticks lying there in the dirt.

This time the bundle was tied with the same ribbon Stephen had used in his bouquet. He was flattered his friend liked the ribbon.

That evening, he hurried about town, looking for living flowers or other items from his small world he could share with this person in the forest. He decided to walk into the forest the following morning and return to the boulder. This time, he'd stay there until his friend arrived.

So the next morning, just after sunrise, Stephen got out of his bed, slinked out the door, and set a course for the forest. The cool morning fog wound its way through the valleys, looking like a flat white snake licking at the tops of the trees.

Stephen clutched his gift — a collection of flowers, with a couple strings and bits of wood wrapped up with the ribbon — and strutted toward the forest. When he made his way up the gradual incline to the boulder, Stephen noticed a small difference.

Next to the boulder, there was a small stump. It

was the perfect size for Stephen, serving as a step up for him to reach the flat top of the boulder.

Stephen looked around as he approached the large stone. Did someone see him the first time he came here? Stephen's eye scoured the woods, which were turning brown with the season. The diverse palette of early autumn in Appalachia was decaying into the monochrome of late autumn.

He couldn't make anything out. No lurking figure. No peering eyes.

Dead leaves crunched and shuffled as Stephen stepped forward. He lifted himself onto the stump and reached out and put his urban bouquet on the flat top of the boulder. The pool of water was still there, a little smaller now. The water was so still that it reflected the swaying treetops that towered above.

Stephen stood on the stump for a moment and then stepped down. He walked slowly over to a large tree and sat in a pile of leaves at its base. The leaves were cool and somewhat damp, and Stephen hoped he wouldn't have to sit there for long. He pulled his knees to his chest and settled in, gazing into the deep, decaying woods for any signs of movement.

The morning warmed up as the sun climbed its way over the mountaintops and banished the fog. Stephen sat in the leaves, nearly motionless, as the sun rose and the shadows shifted around him.

After a while longer and a little more anxiety spreading in his chest, Stephen thought he saw a change in the air straight ahead. He'd seen air do that before, when it gets real hot during the summer, where waves seem to ripple in mid-air.

That's just what it looked like now, but it wasn't nearly hot enough for that. As the air wavered, a figure started to take shape.

It was a small man, cloaked in black with his hands in his pockets. He walked slowly through the carpet of dead leaves. He had his head down, his curly dark hair hanging in front of his face.

The wind seemed to pick up as the man got closer

to Stephen, and Stephen felt his cheeks turning red and ruddy with windburn.

As the man reached the boulder, the wind suddenly stopped. He took his eyes off the ground for the first time as he peered over at the large rock. His gaze fell on the bundle of flowers and sticks. A meek smile formed, and then he turned his gaze to Stephen.

As he made eye contact with the stranger, Stephen felt a wave of melancholy spread through him. It was a comfortable kind of feeling, though, one that seemed to wrap around him like a thick blanket. Part of him felt like he'd always known this person.

Stephen was so lost in his thoughts he didn't notice the man walk over to him.

The two of them were eye-to-eye, but Stephen couldn't quite discern what color the man's eyes were. They seemed to be a hazy, foggy mix of brown and green. They stood out from his pale, young face. His skin was flawless and milky white. The eyes looked like bright swimming pools on the face of a full moon.

"Hello, Stephen," he said.

The words danced into Stephen's ears and he relaxed. His nerves felt like the strings on a violin being tuned down.

"I've enjoyed your gifts," the man said. "Your town must be very beautiful."

Stephen's mind clawed its way through a fog and found words.

"I don't think it's beautiful at all."

"You don't like it? Why is that?"

"I don't belong there. I don't belong anywhere."

"Everybody belongs somewhere."

Stephen considered this. He shook his head.

"Not me. There's no place for little boys who killed their mothers to be happy."

"How did you kill your mother?"

"My living. By being born. My father told me so."

A lump formed in his throat. The man closed his eyes and breathed deeply through his nose.

The lump drifted back down Stephen's throat.

Stephen's eyes shut.

He thought they were only closed for a moment, but when he opened his eyes he realized the sun had moved. Instead of the shadows facing away from him, they faced toward him.

It was a few seconds before Stephen realized his new friend had taken his hands from the pockets of his cloak and now held one of Stephen's hands. The hands were warm, even hot, against Stephen's skin. The boy looked down and felt a pang of alarm at what he saw.

The man's warm hands were a bright red.

Stephen couldn't quite place the shade of red until later, but he would eventually identify it as the hue of a burn. He and his father, as they tended the kettle over the fire, had both burned themselves in moments of carelessness. It was a bizarre, frightening sensation, and often lingered for days.

This man's hands looked as if they had been evenly burned, and that there had been no blistering or scarring. The hands looked weathered and maybe a bit leathery, but they carried no overt signs of trauma or damage.

The man's warmth spread from his hands to Stephen's hand and then slowly through Stephen's whole body. He felt tired but secure, like he did on a dark winter night when he was wrapped up in bed; the world was cold but he was warm.

Stephen's eyes worked their way back up to the man's face, and he was again startled.

The man's eyes were open and vacant. Silent tears fell from the eyes and rolled down his cheeks. Like his hands, the tears were a deep red.

Stephen was reminded of a time a nail in the fence had sliced through his forearm when he was younger. Dark, sticky blood had hurried out of the gash, staining his arm and matting his short arm hair.

The man's tears weren't thick, but they were the same color. They looked like they'd been drawn from a freshly-tapped vein.

They rolled slowly down his face, leaving a light track like legs left in a glass of red wine.

"Mister?" Stephen asked. "Are you alright?"

The man's eyes regained their focus, locking with Stephen's. His expression quickly grew soft.

"I'm just fine, Stephen."

He leaned forward and whispered.

"You have so much sadness inside you. So much loneliness."

Stephen felt like the man's eyes were gazing *through* his own, looking somewhere deep inside him.

"I can help with that," the man said. "I can help with your sorrow. I've heard you, Stephen. I've felt you. In the darkest hours of the night I've sensed you calling out for a friend, for anyone to share your time with.

"I want you to know you're not alone. You're not the only one who feels that way. I felt that way for a long, long time."

Emotions swirled within Stephen. It was as if part of his own soul had written the words this man was saying.

At the same time, this was confusing and even a little frightening. Who was this man? Who were these others? How had this man known what Stephen was feeling and thinking?

"Mister," Stephen said, pulling his head away. "I don't know who you are. How can I trust you to help me?"

The man smiled, the fissures of his dimples pushing around the fading tracks of his tears.

"You'll trust me. I'll prove myself to you. Let's keep seeing each other, alright? Maybe tomorrow?"

Stephen tried to put on a skeptical face.

"Maybe," he said, knowing he'd come back.

The man seemed to know, too. His smile grew a little broader, showing off a set of small, dark teeth.

"Well, you think about it and maybe I'll see you tomorrow."

With that, the man stood and turned to walk away. Stephen watched as the stranger took a couple slow steps, his long black cloak swirling around his legs.

"Mister!" Stephen cried out.

The man turned, a small smile still on his face.

"What's your name? What should I call you?"

The man's smile faded.

"You can call me whatever you'd like, Stephen. I've never had a name."

He turned away again, swishing and crunching his way through the fallen leaves as he strode past the boulder and into the trees.

Like a mirage, the man seemed to fade away into the brown decay of the autumn forest.

And once again, Stephen Marquardt was alone.

***

Stephen came back, as he knew he would, to the boulder in the forest the next day. He couldn't articulate why, exactly, but he didn't have any friends and his father was out of the house once again.

The man with red hands again sat with Stephen and cried heavy red tears as the leaves swirled around them and the shadows bent with the fast-moving sun. Once again, Stephen felt cloaked in warmth as the man knelt beside him and held Stephen's hand.

Stephen skipped school the next day to return to the forest. When they had sat there and Stephen had blissfully swayed in and out of consciousness for the entire morning, the man stopped crying and looked Stephen in the eye.

"Stephen, you know you won't be able to come spend all your days here," he said. "You must go to school. Aren't there people there who will miss you?"

Stephen shook his head. He was thinking about what it would be like to totally abandon the community he felt had abandoned him, and to spend all his time in the forest and the mountains with his new friend. The idea scared him, but he felt a surge of excitement burst within him every time he thought about it.

"I don't want to be there anymore." he said.

"You won't at least try?" the man said.

"But when will we see each other?" Stephen asked.

He felt the lump starting to rise in his throat again. Finally he had found a friend, and the friend was ready to abandon him already.

"We can find time," the man said.

Stephen sat, stunned in his sadness, for a few moments. The man stood, avoiding eye contact. He turned away, his cloak tossing leaves about his feet.

"Wait," Stephen said.

The man froze and looked tentatively over his shoulder.

"Would you be able to come to me?" Stephen asked. "Maybe after school?"

The man stood silently for a moment, considering this.

"Where would we meet?" he asked.

"What about my house?" Stephen asked. "My father is a heavy sleeper. He often comes back from the pub, falls into his bed, and is out cold until the morning. I don't think he'll notice if you come in."

The man was nearly blushing by the time Stephen was done.

"I think that could work well," he said. "Go to school tomorrow, and then perhaps I'll come by at night."

He disappeared into the woods again, and Stephen felt like he was floating down the mountain. The next day and a half was agonizing, as he struggled to sleep that night and then waited impatiently for school to end the next day.

Stephen raced home and paced through the small hut waiting for nightfall. The days were getting shorter, but he still circled his home dozens of times before sunset. His father got home a little earlier than expected — but every bit as drunk as usual, if not more so.

Stephen's father didn't bother to acknowledge his son as he tossed the door open and stumbled through. He leaned heavily against the wall, using it as a crutch to help him to his small bedroom. In one motion, he belched, spat, and flopped facedown on his bed. Then the house went silent except for the crackling of the dying fire.

Stephen's heart raced as he strained his ears to listen through the door. There were no footsteps, but suddenly there was a soft knocking at the door. Stephen sat up, not sure if the sound he heard was really someone knocking. He made his way to the door. He cast a glance back toward his father's bedroom to make sure he hadn't risen at the sound. Of course he hadn't.

The night was dark, but Stephen could tell there was a figure outside the door through the cracks in the wood. He eased the door open, and the man with red hands loomed over him. His round, pale face was like a full moon embedded in his black cloak.

"May I come in?" he asked softly.

Stephen nodded and stepped backward. He gestured for the man to come in. The man stepped over the threshold, bringing a cold night breeze with him. He looked around at the house, a small smile coming to his lips. He brought his hands out of his pockets, more orange than red in the firelight, and folded them under his chin. He closed his eyes and took a deep breath through his nose.

For the first time, Stephen felt a pang of worry about inviting this man into his home. He brushed it aside. This was his friend. And he made him feel like he belonged and like he mattered.

Stephen retreated to his bed and sat on the edge. The man opened his eyes and followed. He sat on the opposite side of the bed from Stephen, facing the fireplace.

He gazed at the fire for a few moments before turning to Stephen, who had lay down and gotten under his blanket. Stephen held out his hand.

Wordlessly, the man with red hands put his hands around Stephen's hand. Stephen noticed the fingers and nails seemed longer than they had been before. His curiosity and anxiety quickly slipped away, though, as he felt a wave of warmth crash over him.

The man breathed deeply. Stephen felt his eyes close, and when he reopened them he noticed the fire was dying down and the man was again crying red tears. They blazed in the dim firelight.

Stephen felt his eyes close again, and he drifted into the darkness of the night.

***

Stephen woke up late, noticing it was already bright

outside. He was alone in the room, and looked around to see there was no sign of his friend's visit. He did notice that his father's work clothes were still on the table.

Stephen dragged himself out of bed and stumbled to his father's room. He walked in to notice that his father was still there on the bed. The room was heavy with an overwhelming stench. His father often stank, especially after drinking too much and soiling himself, but this was even worse than usual.

"Father?" Stephen croaked, waving his hand in front of his face and grimacing. "Father? I think you're late for work."

There was no response. Stephen walked over and shook his shoulder gently. When that didn't rouse his father, Stephen looked closer and noticed he wasn't breathing. He jumped on his father's bed and looked into his face.

Half his face was purple, where the stagnant blood had gathered. Stephen didn't need to check his father's pulse to know he was dead.

The drinking finally caught up with him, Stephen thought to himself. Kneeling on the bed, Stephen didn't even try to stop the tears. He hated his father, but he was still his father. They only had each other, although neither had ever acknowledged it out loud.

Stephen heard from others that his father wasn't always like this. He wasn't always a mean drunk. He was a kind, contributing member of the village before his wife died. Before Stephen killed her.

Cradling his head in his hands, Stephen thought about all he had done. He'd turned his mother into a corpse and his father into a drunk. And now the drunk was a corpse.

Stephen sobbed until his body hurt and his throat was coarse. Then he lay next to his father and stared at the ceiling. He couldn't tell if time was moving quickly or slowly as he lay there. It didn't matter. Time was meaningless to him now.

After a while, Stephen stood and walked to the front room and looked around. He didn't know what he was looking for, and he didn't find it. He kept walking, out the door and into the street.

Without thinking, Stephen turned toward the mountains. He walked slowly, his feet taking control of the rest of his body. He didn't have anybody else to talk with. It had only been a few hours, but he wanted to see the man with red hands again. Maybe he could take some of this pain away, even if it's just for a little while.

***

As Stephen approached the boulder in the woods, he saw the man sitting atop it.

His black cloak stood out against the dull white of the large stone. The contrast of the man's red hands against the stone was even more noticeable.

"I could feel you coming," the man said as Stephen approached. "You're carrying more sorrow than usual."

Stephen collapsed at the man's feet, a fresh bout of sobs thrashing his body. After a few moments, he looked through tears to see a red hand extended in front of his face.

"I want to take you somewhere," the man said. "I've seen your home, now I'd like you to see where I'm from."

Stephen wiped tears away from his face and nodded his head. He reached out and held the man's hand. He immediately felt relief starting to surge through him. The man breathed in deeply, his body shuddering a bit as he did so.

Stephen drifted out of consciousness for a moment, and when he came to, he found he and the man were at the mouth of a cave. They were still in the forest, and it looked like they were still on the mountain.

"Stephen, I know your father is dead. I know how alone you feel."

Stephen shook his head.

"No you don't," he said.

The man knelt and was face-to-face with Stephen.

"I was alone for longer than you can imagine," he breathed. "See, Stephen, I am not of your world. I am of your *earth*, but not of your *world*.

"I was born deep in the ground. So deep that I was

on the border of where the ground is cold and where it's hot."

Stephen looked at the man's hands. *So red they looked like they had been burned.*

"And then people like your father came. They dug deep into the earth. Their greed overpowered their caution. They dug too deeply, all the way to me. Suddenly, I who was alone for generations was released into your world.

"I found that I was drawn to people of your kind who felt alone, who felt abandoned. I could feel their suffering from far away, and could draw them to me. Like you, Stephen. We were drawn to each other.

"Your suffering, your loneliness, your sorrow, they all dwarf what I've felt from others."

Fresh tears came to Stephen's eyes as he thought about being so sad and lonely.

"Stephen, it's not such a horrible thing. You have an unmatched capacity to feel. You're more human than any human I've seen. And I want you to stay. I want us to help each other. You see, when you let me touch you or be around you, your loneliness passes from you to me. *You keep me alive, Stephen.*"

Stephen didn't know what to think. Part of him felt a perverse pride in being so important to somebody. Part of him wanted to run.

"Where do you want me to stay?" Stephen asked, his voice shaking. "Here? In the forest? In this cave?"

He felt more afraid with every word he said. He was starting to regret coming back to the woods.

"Yes, Stephen. I want you to stay here with me. You and I will be friends here for a long time."

"Will I ever get to leave if I end up becoming happy?"

The man smiled, showing those small, dark teeth again.

"If you end up being happy, sure," he said.

Stephen looked into the darkness of the cave.

"Take a look around, if you want," the man said. He put his hand on Stephen's back and guided him gently forward.

Stephen walked slowly into the cave, his footsteps echoing off the wet walls. Again, it felt like his feet were making decisions for the rest of his body as they carried him forward.

The sunlight illuminated the front part of the cave, which included a couple piles of black cloaks and baskets of herbs and sticks. This certainly appeared to be the man's home.

Stephen thought he saw some kind of marking on the wall of the cave. He walked over to it, not noticing that the man was no longer next to him.

As he got closer, Stephen realized what the marks were and his stomach dropped. He held up his hand to the marks and traced them with his fingers. Fingernails had made these marks. Fingernails on small hands.

Stephen turned to the entrance of the cave. The man was standing outside, the red tracks of tears clear on his face.

"Thank you, Stephen. I have a feeling you'll be my favorite one yet."

Stephen ran toward the opening, but a huge stone rolled in front of the cave's mouth. Stephen slammed his fists against it, pushing with all his might. In the small amount of light still getting through the cave's opening, Stephen saw scratch marks all over the boulder.

He collapsed on the ground, sobbing and leaning against the boulder. He had never felt so alone, so hopeless.

After a few moments, he started to feel better. He felt warm, relaxed even. He ran his hand over the cool rock of the boulder, knowing that on the other side, two red hands were there to take his pain away.

"Abandoned" by Sonali Roy

Doppelgängers
Simon MacCulloch

The dream people, memories made actors to play
Those self-serving dramas that shadow the day
To do the undone and to say the unsaid
Are restless as spectres, unliving, undead
Sloughed off in the night like the skin that we shed.

Perhaps, like our tissue, each figment contains
The stamp of our being, the print of our brains
Which, if it could somehow be cultured to grow
Might burgeon to recreate all that we know.
What wisdom might such an edition bestow?

The study of dreams is an imperfect science
A method too curt in its placid reliance
On primitive symbols, reductive dissection
When nurture and nourishment, care and protection
Might yet see the dream folk evolve to perfection.

An Old Fireplace
Jade Jiao

William had slopped down himself again. He insisted, much to Isabel's irritation, on feeding himself his own mush. The other carers had remarked on how they admired him for it. The old boy refused to give into his infirmity, would not sacrifice his dignity, would be dragged kicking and screaming, when the time came, *into that good night*. Except it wasn't up to him, thought Isabel. He could protest all he liked, but infirmity had claimed him, and there was nothing he could do about it. Refusing to let her feed him, just meant that she would have to wash his shirt again. It made more work.

She sighed as she scooped up what she could of the food lying on his chest and took the tray away. Isabel hated old people. She had *always* hated them, she suspected, ever since she had been a little girl. She had detested being forced to kiss her great grandma Mildred on the occasion of her hundredth birthday, when the old bird had had no concept of what day it was or what was happening, and feeling the sagging, wrinkled jowls of her cheek against her lips. She had despised the deafness of her great uncle Max, who had to be told everything five times before he understood, and then would forget it two minutes later anyway. And even now, as a supposedly kind, empathetic, normal adult, she found old people frustrating to be around. No, more than frustrating. She found them scary, in the way she found drunks or drug addicts to be scary, because old people – most of them – were *loose cannons*. You never knew what mad thing they might say or do next, because with every passing year, they grew in senility. And what was worse, a lot of the time, you couldn't tell which ones were still holding onto their sanity, and which ones were *full blown cuckoo*. She knew it was terribly wrong to feel this way. And so, she told no one.

It was a terrible irony then, that her current place of employ just so happened to be a residential home for the elderly and infirm. A stop gap job. A few months to tide her over before she found something more suited to her particular temperament. But then 1971 had turned to 1972. '72 had turned to '73. Before she knew it, she was thirty, largely unskilled, and had three years of experience flipping over old men in bed and changing wet sheets.

"Isabel," said the manager, catching her as she exited the kitchen. "One of the girls who does our night shifts has had to leave unexpectedly. I wouldn't normally ask, but would you fancy covering tomorrow? It'd be 10pm through to 6. Easy money – you mainly just have to make sure none of them have escaped through the front door."

"I don't know. I've got the children at home," Isabel replied.

"It's time and a half. And your oldest must be almost a teenager now. She'll be alright to manage, won't she? I really think you'd prefer nights. Less interaction."

Isabel bit the inside of her cheek in contemplation. "I wouldn't ask," said the manager, "But I *really* need someone."

After some further hesitation, Isabel accepted. She couldn't very well say no. At the scheduled time, she arrived at the home under the cover of darkness, with the foreboding feeling of being somewhere she shouldn't. Of being an intruder. She entered and made her way to the break room through the dim, gloomy entrance. It was amazing how the same space, at a different time of day, could feel so wholly different. A place of mundanity and mild annoyance had turned unfamiliar. One might almost venture to spooky. The home was an old-fashioned place anyway (she supposed this was on purpose to make the residents feel more at one with the surroundings) but now it truly looked like a bonafide haunted house. It was eerie. Hushed. Unpleasant. She moved quickly and tried not to dwell on her thoughts.

Janet, a senior carer who had worked at the home for most, if not all, of her working life, was already sitting in the break room, eating a biscuit and flipping through a magazine. The evening shift workers completed their final tasks, gathered their things, and left. Isabel made herself and Janet a cup of tea each, and then went to check everyone was still in bed. The home wasn't overly large, currently holding ten residents, and so the check didn't take long. When she saw that all her charges were sound asleep, she returned to the break room and put her feet up. Every thirty minutes, she and Janet would take it in turns to go on a round. Soon enough, Isabel was wondering why she hadn't been doing nights this whole time. It was *so* much easier. No feedings. No boring, repetitive conversations. No snippy, overly-critical family members visiting. Just peace.

"It's much easier until something goes wrong," warned Janet. "Then it's much worse than days. But, fingers crossed, everyone sleeps through until morning."

At 1am, it was Isabel's turn to make another round. The house cat, Tabitha, had been stretched languorously on a cushion in the corner since eleven, but jumped up with an impeccable sense of duty as she arose. She slipped between Isabel's ankles to follow her with a satisfied purr. Together, they headed up the stairs and checked each of the bedrooms in turn. Everything was silent, save for the ticking of the grandfather clock in the hall, and the snoring of the residents. The final room belonged to Alma Quinn, a docile, sleepy woman with no remaining relatives (or none who cared to visit). Isabel looked through the cracked door. Alma wasn't there.

She wasn't worried. Alma had probably managed to take herself to the toilet. She went and knocked on the toilet door and waited, but there was no response.

"Alma, are you in there?"

She pushed on the door and it opened, unlocked. Empty.

Still, no cause for alarm. Anyone who had worked with old people could tell you they liked to go for a wander. They often forgot where they were, and tried to go home, or to find a family member. The exterior doors were all secured, so there was little chance of an escape. Isabel made her way downstairs and through to the sitting room.

The sitting room, the central hub of activity during the day, was dimly lit and lonely now. Thick curtains were drawn over the windows, and everything sat still and silent. Isabel walked in nervously, as though she had no right to be there. Tabitha the cat cautiously followed, then stopped suddenly. Her ears flattened, and she tucked her previously loose, extended tail between her legs.

"Come on, Tabby," said Isabel, speaking only to break the silence, but the cat turned and skittered away, vanishing with a hiss. Shrugging, Isabel moved to continue her hunt for Alma, when she noticed something and came to a halt. Over the back of the armchair closest to the fireplace, some black hair was just visible, peeking out over the top rail. The sight of it turned Isabel's blood cold. *Who was that?* Nobody at the home, nobody who *should be* at the home, had hair like that. The chair creaked as the person sitting there shifted slightly and Isabel's heart lurched. She wanted to run to get Janet, but then –

"Who's there?" came a small, scratchy voice.

Isabel took a deep, shaking breath and moved to see Alma was the person in the chair. The black hair must have been some shadow, or an illusion, because now she saw only Alma's scant white tresses. She wore a blue and white floral nightie and looked tiny and shrunken, the contours and caverns of her skeletal face thrown into shadow. Her watery blue eyes were trained intently in front of her.

"Alma, you frightened me. Let's take you back to bed." Isabel reached out a hand to take the old lady by the shoulder, but Alma shrugged it off, keeping her eyes forward.

"She's in there. In the fireplace," whispered Alma, staring at the hearth, laser-focussed enough to bore a hole in it. Isabel turned to trace Alma's gaze. She saw no one.

"Nobody's in there," said Isabel. "Let's go to bed. It's late."

"She's in there. She wants me to get in, too. I've told her I can't fit."

"*Who's* in there?" asked Isabel. "There's nobody."

She didn't want to admit it to herself, but Alma was scaring her. She wanted to rip all six and a half, frail, tiny stones of the crone out of that chair and carry her up to bed. To leave her tucked up and not see her again until the sun had risen. But she persisted with her act of patience and kindness. It was what she was being paid for, after all.

"You can see her. She's looking at you," said Alma. "She doesn't like that you've seen her. She'll make it so that never happens again, believe you me."

Isabel felt a thousand tiny pinpricks move over her back. She didn't want to turn around again. She kept her back to the fireplace, and her eyes cemented on Alma's.

"Stop it," she said. "I don't like what you're saying. It's nonsense."

"Look."

From behind her came a dull thud. Isabel jumped. It was followed by another. Banging inside the fireplace. Something in the chimney, beating on the brickwork, its drumming echoing up and down through the house.

"Look," repeated Alma.

Slowly, Isabel turned to the fireplace. She recoiled. Something black was sticking out from the darkness of the chimney. Black and shiny. Her stomach flipped and she wanted to scream, but her throat wouldn't cooperate, and she was unable to make any noise. Unable to move. She watched in wide-eyed horror as the thing in the chimney started to shake and laugh at her. A loud, hateful witch's laugh that bellowed and filled her ears.

At that moment, Janet rushed into the room. She went straight past Isabel and to the fireplace, bending down underneath it so that her head was looking up into the flume. She was muttering something expletive-laden to herself, her hands reaching up into the darkness. With a clang, she pulled out the heavy metal grate that blocked the entrance to the chimney and dropped it into the dusty hearth. With it, fell a large black shape. Some oily, amorphous thing that rolled forward onto the floor. Isabel drew back, and realised she was gripping Alma's arm much too tightly, but Alma didn't move. Isabel couldn't figure out what she was looking at for a few seconds, and adrenaline pumped hard in her veins, making her head throb.

"Bloody crows. As soon as I heard the banging I knew. It's happened before," said Janet through gritted teeth.

It was a crow. The thing must have fallen into the chimney from the roof. It was enormous, twitching and spasming in shock, its wing bent at an odd angle and clearly broken beyond repair. It hadn't been laughter that she'd heard, but cawing. She knew instinctively that the bird was dying. It took increasingly longer pauses now between its shrieks, the sound becoming fainter and weaker. Janet bent down and tenderly lifted the bird In her arms. It did nothing to resist. Making a soft cooing over it, she swiftly snapped its neck to the side. Its head flopped down strangely, like the limb of an abandoned marionette.

"Nothing else to do but to put it out of its misery," said Janet. "I'll dispose of it. You take Alma to her room." Janet was a tough lady. Capable. Isabel was incredibly glad and grateful to be with her.

Alma, broken from her trance, rose from the armchair with a groan and, supported by Isabel, began to shuffle out and down the corridor. They took the small lift up, then Alma climbed into bed, lying flat on her back.

"Goodnight, Alma," said Isabel. With the tips of her fingers, she picked up the edge of a blanket and brought it to the old lady's chin. "Try to stay in here until morning. I think there's been enough excitement for one night."

Alma didn't respond, so Isabel flicked off the light and went back to the break room. Janet was in there scrubbing her hands with soap and hot water. "Bloody things are so greasy," she said. "Disgusting."

"That scared me half to death," said Isabel. "It was really bad timing."

"What do you mean?"

"Just before the crow fell down, Alma was babbling about someone being up the chimney. It was weird... Has she ever said something to you about someone being in the fireplace?"

Janet paused and looked up from the sink. "You

don't know the story, then," she said.

Isabel shook her head. Janet came and sat across the table from her. She leant forward conspiratorially. "Alma lived here when she was a young girl. This building used to be a normal family home, right up until about twenty years ago, when it was sold and converted to run as a care business.

"Now, this is how the story was told to me by the old cook who was here before you started. The story goes that Alma had an older sister, I don't know her name, but apparently she wasn't a well girl. She was about ten years older and, I don't know all the details because this is probably a fourth or fifth-hand account, but she wasn't quite right in the head. Maybe a bit slow? Or troubled. I'm not sure. Anyway, one rainy day, Alma and her sister were playing hide-and-seek in the house, and this sister somehow manages to climb up the sitting room chimney. She comes to a bend, designed to stop smoke from coming back down into the room, and although she's a tall girl, tries to contort herself around it. She gets stuck. And in the soot and the dark, she suffocates and dies, and by all accounts, the family doesn't find her body for quite some time, and only then because of the smell."

"That's horrific," said Isabel. "I wish you hadn't told me."

"So, every now and again when it's late, Alma seems to remember this and wants to sit by the fire. Sometimes she'll say her sister is still up there. The joys of the night shift, eh? But the crow coming down just as Alma's about to scare the pants off you, *that's a new one*, that's really the cherry on the cake. One day, when I'm retired and you're sat here with some wee slip of a thing, you can tell them that and really terrify them."

I won't be sitting here by then, Isabel thought resentfully, *I'll be somewhere new with no old people.* But she smiled and nodded, trying to get her heart rate back to normal, and to release the tension she'd accumulated. The rest of the shift was uneventful, and at 6am, she was relieved of her duty and went home. The story Janet had told her was disturbing, but she reasoned that it probably wasn't entirely true, if indeed true at all.

When she next returned to work on her usual morning shift, and the house was once again drab and familiar, she took a seat next to Alma. It was a glorious day. Sunshine poured in through the sitting room's open windows, letting in the sound of bees and birdsong. Tabitha had taken a seat on the old lady's lap and purred gently, kneading her paws into the arm of the chair.

"How are you today?" Isabel asked.

Alma looked at her from behind tired, glazed eyes, showing barely a semblance of recognition. Isabel thought of her blank, lost grandma Mildred, and inwardly shuddered.

"Is it true you lived in this house before? When you were a young girl?" she continued.

At that, Alma perked up a bit. She nodded. "Yes, my family owned this house. My mother and father both died just after the Great War, and it was sold then. But I was living with my husband and had children of my own at that time. We made a wonderful home together. We had big beautiful hydrangeas. Blue and pink and purple, they were."

"Did you have brothers and sisters?" Isabel prodded.

"Oh yes, I had Albert, my younger brother, and Margaret. She never married. She was a nurse. And then there was the other one." A funny look came over Alma's face, and she patted her lips together and began fidgeting with a button on her cardigan.

"The other one?"

"She had the most lovely black hair. You know her," Alma said.

"I do?" asked Isabel. She felt suddenly as though they were the only two people in the room. The other residents, guests, and members of staff seemed to melt away to nothing in the bright sunlight. Only Alma and her voice remained.

"She's the one in the chimney." Alma gestured in the direction of the fireplace. Despite the sunlight, Isabel shivered.

"Not anymore," she said. "Once, she might have been, but that was a long time ago. She isn't there anymore, Alma."

"She's there," said Alma, and patted Isabel reassuringly on the hand with her own cold, wrinkled paw, as though reassuring a child. "She's come back for me. It's almost my time. You'll see. She won't let you off so easy, either, I don't think. She doesn't like you."

Isabel stood up, and the other people and their chatter returned to her, once again filling the room. She stepped away from Alma, who smiled at her vacantly. The old bat didn't know what she was talking about, Isabel told herself. She went and got on with some cleaning and other jobs elsewhere.

Over the next few weeks, she stuck to day shifts. She fancied a few times that she could hear a faint scraping in the chimney, but on the one occasion she had gathered her courage and stuck her head under the grate to peer upwards, she had seen nothing but black. She'd heard the wind whistling softly down, and felt the cool breeze from above, but had seen no sign of anything else. She told herself it was probably a mouse somewhere, or pipes in the walls.

The trouble didn't start again until Isabel's next night shift, when she noticed something disquieting. She had made her regular rounds and found everyone to be in bed, asleep. As she wandered back through the main entrance hall, she noticed something on the floor. She bent down for a closer examination. A series of long, black marks streaked the floorboards. She ran her finger along the one closest to her, and realised it was soot. A grimy, coal footprint. A trail of them, coming from the sitting room and leading along the floor and up the stairs. No – they *had* been leading up the stairs, but there was a second set, she observed, leading *back down*. Whoever had left the footprints was currently to be found in the sitting room. Filled with dread. Isabel followed the prints, heart beating fast, frightened but intrigued.

She entered the room and her eyes went straight to the fireplace. She gasped. Over the hearth, two veined, white legs were sticking out. Isabel froze. The feet weren't touching the floor. They dangled in the darkness, then slowly began to rise. There was a horrible scraping noise from within the chimney, and the feet were drawn upwards, inch by inch, like the body of a helpless rodent being drawn into the chewing, crunching, hungry maw of a snake, until they completely vanished. Isabel screamed. She turned and ran.

She burst into the break room. Janet, alarmed, pushed back her chair, almost spilling her tea. Isabel was hysterical. Blinding tears streamed over her cheeks and she screeched like a woman possessed. She gabbled, half nonsensically to Janet, who ran to the sitting room to see what was happening for herself. There, she found Alma, slumped dead on the floor near the hearth. Her face had turned blue, her mouth hung open, and her eyes were turned almost to the back of her head, sockets rolled up into the darkness of the chimney. Heart failure. Nothing to be done about it but to ring the proper authorities.

Isabel didn't try again to tell anyone what she'd seen. Who would believe her? What would it achieve? She didn't work any more night shifts, and handed in her notice at the residential home within the fortnight. No more old people. No more of that horrible old house. She found work in a nice, fluorescently-lit, normal shop. She clocked off before 6pm every day, and all was well with the world.

After one particularly long day, she came home and set the tea things on the table. Her feet were aching, and she wanted nothing more than to sit down undisturbed, but her youngest came to her and tugged at her jumper.

"What's wrong?" she asked, only half paying attention, and thinking more about when she would have time to go shopping for eggs and bread and packed lunches.

"I think there's someone in the front room," her son whispered. "In the fireplace."

Her veins turned icy, and she looked down at his large, tear-filled eyes. Silently, she crept to the living room door, and opening it a tiny crack, looked into the darkness towards the fireplace.

From the chimney, she heard a faint scratch and flutter.

"Untitled" by Naomi Sheely

ARTICLE

Treating the Supernatural, the Mysterious, the Occult, and the Weird with the writings of Arthur Machen...
Sonali Roy

      The presence of the weird and supernatural in literature is nothing new, but the fact is that its persistent popularity attests its existence aligned to the socio-psychological basis. Maybe, the term 'weird' arouses some mysterious feelings, or we cannot just imagine anything mysterious without the supernatural- say of some spectral or eerie sounds, or some hallucinations- all these satisfy the mysterious criteria to its full brim. A story enjoys the glory as while touched up by such mysterious elements like the fairy, an alien, apparitions, or some other otherworldly phenomena. Readers love reading the unmortal, or maybe wordsmiths enjoy incorporating the mystery through the unmortal, devils, angels, myths, gods, goddesses, magicians, witches, wonderland, or the UFO. Maybe, the appeal springs from the demand as every living creature is mortal, and that all of us want to have some temporary escape from the difficulties, crisis, and tragedies we suffer from. Ah, we are all humans! And this is human psychology that paves the way to supernaturalism- may be it's real or absurd- maybe, we have some relevant experiences or not. Whatever it might be, we relish while we read the unearthly elements. And here, mystery gets compacted.

A versatile talent, Arthur Machen, contributed as a literary figure, journalist, and an actor though flourished as an influential writer of the supernatural, fantasy, and horror fiction.

Living in between 1863 and 1947, Machen came of a family of a clergyman of a church of England as Arthur Llewellyn Jones. Jones used his mother Janet's family name 'Machen' as his pen name. During his youth, Machen went through a variety of genres including, but not limited to the classics of the Greek and the Roman, the Elizabethan and the Jacobean dramatists, and his contemporaries, especially Charles Dickens. In his father's library, Machen enjoyed the *Arabian Nights*, pages by Sir Walter Scott, DeQuincey, Tennyson, and the Brontes. When he was eight, Machen formed fascination for *Don Quixote*. And just at the age of 12, he became a thorough reader of the *Pickwick Papers, Confessions of an English Opium-Eater, The Heart of Midlothian, Gargantua and Pantagruel*, and leaves involving the romance, remote places, and fairy.

Though always holding on Christian beliefs, Machen had the fascination for mysticism, paganism, and Hermeticism. And these later developed his interests for supernaturalism and occult. Folkloristic legends and traditions as relevant to Wales's landscape and history strengthened Machen's Celtic background, and he got naturally inclined towards the world of supernaturalism that he recurrently employed throughout his literary endeavors. His love for his native Monmouthshire, Wales, where he grew up in the midst of the stunning landscapes, medieval castles, and the Roman ruins, is crystal-clear in his autobiography 'Far Off Things', where Machen refers to his native as its Welsh name 'Gwent'.

In the first volume, he says, "I shall always esteem it as the greatest piece of fortune that has fallen to me, that I was born in that noble, fallen Caerleon-on-Usk, in the heart of Gwent [...] for the older I grow the more firmly am I convinced that anything which I may have accomplished in literature is due to the fact that when my eyes were first opened in earliest childhood they had before them the vision of an enchanted land" (A. Machen, Far Off Things, London, Martin Secker, 1922, 15).

But, not only, Wales, Machen had also fascination for London, where he was sent to be trained as a surgeon at the age of 18 though already proved his potential as a wordsmith.

In 1881, Machen published his long poem *Eleusinia* on the Eleusinian Mysteries.

By 1884, Machen started working as a compiler of some obscure literature and a magazine editor for the occult book publisher George Redway. In 1885, with the Silurian background of his native Wales, Machen started working on *The Chronicle of Clemendy*, tales about knights and fair ladies. Although the book did not earn warm reception in England, Machen was welcome, and London became his home. 1885 marked another milestone in Machen's life, as he met with Arthur E. Waite in the British Museum. Apart from his early readings, Machen was influenced much by Waite, "the greatest occultist of his age" (Charles Williams, *The Greater Trumps*, The Noonday Press Edition [New York, 1962], ii.).

During the 1890s, Machen became associated to the Hermetic Order of the Golden Dawn, a London-based 'secret society' that aimed to study and practice the occult and metaphysics. Undoubtedly, the knowledge and training Machen received at the society contributed much in the growth and development for his future writings. And W.B. Yeats was one more popular personality attracted towards the society.

In his first major work 'The Great God Pan' published in the magazine *The Whirlwind* in 1890, Machen portrays the stunning landscapes of Wales, its valleys, and forests, where lots of mysterious occurrings happen, and the neighborhood gets alarmed. Machen's presentation of the rural life throws insights into how the small communities used to live in the Welsh countryside.

At the same time, the subject arrests the mythology and folklore of the place that definitely involves the Roman past and culture- take for the location for the spiritual occurring or the worship for the ancient deity for healing.

With its Roman historical setting, the region and the entire depiction create a perfect atmosphere for the uncanny and the supernatural. In the story, the city of London is also significant that the narrator calls it the "City of Ressurections", although the move from the rural atmosphere of Wales to the built environment of the city may sound odd to some extent, as the Welsh and the English differ a lot in respect to cultural background. But, perhaps, Machen wanted to portray the socio-psychological crisis through the contrasted effect of the rural and the urban. Furthermore, here in the story, the ancient past is juxtaposed with the urban present and the urban with the suburban settings.

Widely popular as a Gothic tale, 'The Great God Pan' written to reflect the state of cultural or moral decline springs from the late 18th century, when people found a sparkling interest in Gothic architecture and medieval settings as characterized by passionate scenes and damsels in distress though Machen's approach of Gothic treatment was completely different that he wanted to present the traditional traits in an unconventional manner. Actually, *The Great God Pan* is an intermingling of commoners, dreams, death, spirits, ghosts, and weird things and objects, speaking of Helen Vaughn, who, since her early age, communicates with the evil spirits. Helen was the daughter to Mary, a beautiful ward to a scientist, who conducted a minor brain surgery on Mary so that she could see beyond the material world. And London critics badly criticized the book as most ridiculous. *The Three Imposters* received the same impression. But, American reviewers encouraged Machen. Most interestingly, he used to save all the reviews of his titles and published a few of them in *Precious Balms* (London, 1924).

Occultism, mysticism, and inclination towards rituals and secrets were somehow odd at the heart of the late Victorian Britain of rationalities and enlightenment though Machen's *The Great God Pan* earned much success for his treatment of occult subjects in the story. Here, a common woman is transformed into demonic form. Machen learned these subjects during his first employment in London, when he worked as a cataloguer. In her book, *The Supernatural in Modern English Fiction*, Dorothy Scarborough puts, "The most revolting instances of suggestive diabolism are found in Arthur Machen's stories, where supernatural science opens the way for the devil to enter the human soul, since the biologist by a cunning operation on the brain removes the moral sense, takes away the soul, and leaves a being absolutely diabolized. Worse still is the hideousness of *Seeing the Great God Pan*, where the daemonic character is a composite of the loathsome aspects of Pan and the devil, from which horrible paternity is born a child that embodies all the unspeakable evil in the world" (Scarborough 1917:139).

Machen's *The Inmost Light* is another story set in the paranormal background taking the readers to the world of horror and the supernatural. Here, Machen creates suspense through characterization and narrative, where a mad doctor Black is seen incarnating the soul of his wife, Agnes, into a jewel emitting radiance.

As a craft man, Machen mentioned in his literary reflections *Hieroglyphics*, "If ecstasy be present, then I say there is fine literature, if it be absent, then, in spite of all the cleverness, all the talents, all the workmanship and observation and dexterity you may show me, then, I think, we have a product (possibly a very interesting one) which is not fine literature" (*Hieroglyphics*, p.17.). He perceived ecstasy as deep love and respect, intense joy, mystery, wonder, and the crave for the unknown that can lead you withdraw from common life, as he said in *The White People and Other Weird Stories*, "Sorcery and sanctity, there are the only realities. Each is an ecstasy of withdrawal from common life." And it is this ecstasy that readers would admire Machen for forever. He incorporated ecstasy in all his works- say of *The Hill of Dreams*, *The Secret Glory*, or *A Fragment of Life*. In his works, Machen exercised his mystic vision- his semi-autobiographical novel *The Hill of Dreams* depicts Lucian Taylor, a young man absorbed in dreams, fantasies, and supernatural experiences and speaks of his dreamy childhood in the countryside background of Wales- here, Machen installed the fictional town on the real town of Caerleon. Lucian tried to live on writing and art, but died with all his dreams unfulfilled. Instead, he received lifelong poverty and suffering. That his efforts were a complete failure is really a pity- rather, it invokes depression that delves deep into our inner world- it's heart-wrenching. The story is all full of Machen's musical prose, mystic vision, artistic taste, and structural style.

John Gunther described Machen thus, "He reminded me of David Lloyd George, the Sphinx, a Benda mask, George Washington, Pan, W. J. Bryan, and his own Lucian in *The Hill of Dreams*. There is grotesquery in his face, and also beauty. Snow white hair, long and thick, cut horizontally in a heavy bob. Clouded blue eyes, very tired. Beautifully kept, waxlike hands. Red, glazed cheeks, which ball up and jeel when he laughs" [Dilly Tante, pseud. (ed. Stanley J. Kunitz), Living Authors (New York, 1937, p. 241.)

In later parts of his life (in 1900 and onwards), Machen was instigated by one of his friends Christopher Wilson and joined Sir Frank Benson's Shakespeare Repertory Company and worked there for nine years. Afterwards, Machen enjoyed the success with the publication of his *The Bowmen and Other Tales of War*. He also played the role of Dr. Johnson at garden parties at his home in St. John's Wood.

In 1927, H. P. Lovecraft penned a critical essay titled as 'Supernatural Horror in Literature', where he interpreted 'The Great God Pan' as a "weird tale" (H. P. Lovecraft, Supernatural Horror in Literature, New York, Dover, 1973, 427)- he established Machen as one of the four (Algernon Blackwood, Lord Dunsany, and M.R. James form parts of the other three in the genre.) "modern masters" of supernatural horror.

Lovecraft's works were substantially influenced by

Machen. Machen's use of contemporary Welsh or London background resulted in Lovecraft's use of a New England background. Besides, Machen influenced magic realism though mystic vision was his main focus.

Further Readings:
https://biography.wales/pdf/s2-MACH-ART-1863.pdf
https://onlinelibrary.wiley.com/doi/abs/10.1111/j.1468-0114.1965.tb06393.x
https://egrove.olemiss.edu/cgi/viewcontent.cgi?article=1415&context=studies_eng_new
https://is.muni.cz/th/qnbjj/BP_Supernatural_elements.pdf
https://www.forgottenbooks.com/en/download/TheSupernaturalinModernEnglishFiction_10000978.pdf
https://academic.oup.com/book/46854/chapter/413755135/chapter-pdf/57464060/oso-9780192843777-chapter-3.pdf
http://dspace.unive.it/bitstream/handle/10579/23754/855193-1257623.pdf?sequence=2
https://www.duo.uio.no/bitstream/handle/10852/88826/1/MVS_master_KULH4890.pdf
https://ora.ox.ac.uk/objects/uuid:dd0d98b7-de95-48c7-9369-814f204a3921
https://www.dukonference.lv/files/proceedings_of_conf/53konf/valodnieciba_literaturzinatne/Semeneca.pdf

ARTICLE

The Bizarre Sis-Boom-Bah of *Bride of the Gorilla*
Denise Noe

This essay is dedicated to John O'Dowd, author of *Kiss Tomorrow Goodbye: The Barbara Payton Story*

Released in 1951, *Bride of the Gorilla* is a cult film. This essay examines why this movie, regarded by no one as a masterpiece, resonates with audiences. Written and directed by Curt Siodmak, who wrote the screenplay for the 1941 classic *The Wolf Man*, *Bride* has a plot line reminiscent of the earlier, unquestionably superior, film. In *Wolf*, Lon Chaney Jr. plays a man who transforms into a wolf. In *Bride*, a man is cursed so that he either transforms – or believes he transforms – into a "sukurat," a beast resembling a gorilla. Chaney also appears in *Bride* but does not play the man-into-beast character.

Compared to the 1941 *Wolf*, *Bride* was filmed on a shoestring budget – and it shows: sets are cheap, the overall look cheesy. Clips from documentaries about jungles are occasionally interspersed into the movie. Indeed, *Bride* opens with scenes of jungle footage and a voiceover telling us this is the story of how "the jungle itself took the law into its own hands." Footage showing a puma, monkey, lizard, leopard, and an anaconda is followed by a view of a wrecked "Van Gelder Manor."

Barbara Payton

Then we see lovely Dina Van Gelder (Barbara Payton) dancing under a ceiling fan in a beautiful Van Gelder Manor. Payton wears a tight fitting sarong that accentuates her curvaceous figure. In Andrew Dowdy's book, *The Films of the Fifties: The American State of Mine*, Dowdy tells of attending an initial showing of the film: "Barbara's appearance onscreen was greeted with instant verbal approval, accompanied by whistling, stomping, and the ecstatic tribute of flying popcorn boxes, many of them sacrificed unemptied." John O'Dowd in his book, *Kiss Tomorrow Goodbye: The Barbara Payton Story,* observes that the above was "an understandable response for Barbara, who, at 24, was a mesmerizing beauty . . . fully displayed here with her long-legged, hourglass figure, sensuous mouth, provocative eyes and flawless skin. That her beauty would elicit such a vociferous reaction was proof enough that film audiences loved the sight of this new, blond bombshell. Indeed, her appearance in *Bride of the Gorilla* proves that in 1951, Barbara Payton was, without question, a Grade-A *knockout*."

After she dances, Barney Chavez (Raymond Burr) enters. A supervisor at the rubber plantation owned by Dina's husband, Barney is dissatisfied with his work, comparing it to slavery. Dina asks, "Aren't we all slaves?" She soon negates her own question, saying, "Not me – I'm free."

Barney says, "A woman like you ought to travel and wear pretty clothes." Dina replies, "My life is here with my husband." Barney asserts, "You're confusing gratitude with love."

Into the mansion come her husband, Klaas Van Gelder (Paul Cavanagh), and Dr. Viet (Tom Conway). The film shows its age when Dr. Viet expresses concern for Dina in bluntly racist terms, saying, "White people shouldn't live too long in the jungle."

Dina and Klaas clasp each other's arms and head for the dining table. Klaas opens the Bible to a passage that begins, "The heart is deceitful above all things." The verse seems appropriate when Klaas mentions the complaint of a worker about Barney's relationship with a young South American Indian woman. Barney has apparently done a love 'em and leave 'em number with Larina (Carol Varga), the daughter of housekeeper Al-Long (Gisela Werbisek). Like Payton, Varga was clearly cast in part as eye candy. Varga is a shapely and beautiful young woman.

Upset that Barney has seduced and abandoned Larina, Klaas orders Barney to leave. Outside Van Gelder Mansion, Larina begs Barney to take her with him. He coldly brushes her off. We soon see Larina complaining to mother Al-Long about Barney's duplicitous ways. Al-Long says, "I warned you to stay with your own people."

A powerful sexual chemistry animates scenes between Barney and Dina. Barney realizes Dina does not want him to leave. A confrontation takes place in the jungle between Barney and Klaas. The more heavily muscled Barney easily lays slightly built Klaas on his back. Then Barney watches nonchalantly as a poisonous snake kills Klaas.

Unknown to Klaas and Barney, they are being watched by Al-Long. Usually seen with a long black scarf accenting her potato head, Al-Long is reminiscent of Maria Ouspenskaya's Gypsy Maleva in *The Wolf Man*. Outraged by Barney's callous abandonment of her daughter and his murder of her employer, the sinister Al-Long casts a spell on him: "Cursed be Barney Chavez. . . . He shall be like an animal. . . . The jungle shall hunt him to his death."

With Klaas barely cold in his grave, Barney marries Dina. At their wedding reception, he suddenly watches one of his hands turn unaccountably hairy. On his wedding night, Barney does not consummate his marriage but runs into the jungle as Dina gazes after him.

In the jungle, Barney watches his hands turn hairy and sees his reflection in water – the reflection of an ape. He is either turning into a gorilla-like creature or believes he is.

We soon see Dr. Viet talking with Police Commissioner Taro – who is played by Lon Chaney Jr. Chaney's role in this film contrasts with his starring role in *Wolf*. Here his role is small but pivotal. Indeed, it was Chaney as Taro that we first heard in the opening voiceover. Taro is a South American Indian who was educated in a white-run system. He often feels alienated from his "own people" and torn between two ways of thinking. In the conversation with Dr. Viet, Taro discusses recent reports of a strange animal in the jungle. Taro then relates the legend of the "sukurat," a "jungle demon" that is really a human being transformed into an animal. The conversation turns to Barney and Taro says, "I know that Barney Chavez murdered Klaas Van Gelder" but acknowledges lacking proof. Taro elaborates, "He cannot escape punishment. Barney Chavez will be brought to justice."

In one scene, the film ambivalently comments on gender roles. Barney and Dina plan to sell Van Gelder Manor. Van Heusen (Paul Maxey) wishes to buy. Van Heusen and Taro are at Van Gelder Manor but Barney is not. Van Heusen fumes about Barney's absence when Van Heusen has brought over the papers to transfer ownership. Taro observes, "Mrs. Chavez can sign the papers. She's the legal owner." However, Dina retorts, "My husband is the boss in this house." Van Heusen says, "I wish my wife could hear that." Dina's retort indicates that she subscribes to traditional sex roles, a common stance in 1951. However, Van Heusen's reply indicates that, even in 1951, sex roles were not rigid with a rough equality, and even wifely dominance, being possible.

A later scene between Barney and Dina has him informing Dina that he will not sell Van Gelder Manor. He tells her he "belongs to the jungle. . . . The animals talk to me. I understand them."

Toward the end of the film, Dina follows Barney into the jungle. Transformed into an aggressive were-ape, Barney attacks Dina. Police shoot him dead. In a final voiceover, Taro somberly declares, "The jungle had risen up to punish Barney Chavez for his crimes."Made on a sadly limited budget and hampered by a mediocre script, *Bride*'s cult status is nevertheless assured. As O'Dowd observes, it is "the second of two films" for which Barbara Payton "will forever be known." (The first film for which Payton is famous is the 1950 crime drama, *Kiss Tomorrow Goodbye*, in which she starred opposite James Cagney.)

Why is *Bride* a cult film? This writer sees several reasons. One is that it is so easily ridiculed. The film has been comically referenced in an episode of the *M*A*S*H* TV series, the *1st Annual Mystery Science Theater 3000 Summer Blockbuster Review, This Movie Sucks!* and elsewhere.

Another reason for its cult film status is the odd way it combines a cheesy atmosphere with excellent performances and depth of meaning.

Raymond Burr plays Barney Chavez with a menacing machismo and an undercurrent of animalistic sensuality perfect for the man-into-beast part. Gisela Werbisek as Al-Long is fascinatingly eerie. Perhaps the most notable performance is that of Barbara Payton who is luminous as the passionate but often frightened and confused Dina.

In this writer's opinion, *Bride* possesses more meaning than its campy title suggests. As a "User Review" at the

Internet Movie Database (IMDB) asserts, "The somewhat sketchy story reads like a medieval legend, the stuff Shakespeare plays like *MacBeth* were made of." This reviewer later observes, "The strangeness of the sets and the seemingly deliberate evasion of authenticity heighten the symbolic significance of the story in an odd sort of way. On the set there is a strong separation between the inside and the outside. Inside, people move about in the usual Hollywood parlor surroundings you can see in numerous movies of that period. Outside, right in front of the parlor window, there is the vicious jungle with its fleshy greenery. Inside, there is civilization or at least a civilized façade. Outside, men become beasts." Another User Review at the IMDB describes the film as having "a lot more to it than you would think at first about crime, justice, and revenge, and makes you think about it, too. More penetrating and thought-provoking than many of the big budgeted films about courts and law that in many cases the criminal gets away with his or her crimes due to a technicality or a smart and skillful lawyer. There are not technicalities or lawyers in the jungle."

There may also be an ugly subtext to this 1951 movie. It is possible it represents a white racist metaphor for sex between blacks and whites. Although the white racist stereotype seeing black people as especially "ape-like" is contrary to fact – simians lack curly hair and thick lips – it is possible the film is informed by such racism. The title card for the film stated: "A blonde and a savage, alone in the jungle . . . Her clothes torn away, screaming in terror . . . Her marriage vows were more than fulfilled!" Dr. Viet's early racist statement, "White people shouldn't live too long in the jungle," may indicate racist underpinnings to the entire plot.

Another reason *Bride* is a cult film might be the way in which it echoes the lives of its stars both before and after its 1951 release. As noted, Lon Chaney Jr. plays in this movie that has a human-into-animal transformation like the one his character endured in *Wolf*.

Bride was not the only time Raymond Burr appeared in an ape-themed film. Three years later, in 1951, he played in *Gorilla At Large*. A cheap and cheesy film like *Bride*, Burr does not transform but works in a circus around a gorilla.

However, the main true-life resonances in *Bride* are with the life of its female star, Barbara Payton. Her riches to rags story is one of the most tragic in Hollywood history. In 1949, Payton earned $10,000 a week for her acting at a time when the average American family income was less than that. By 1963, she was an alcoholic prostitute selling herself for as little as $5.

Payton got her big break co-starring with Lloyd Bridges in the 1949 film noir *Trapped*. Positive reviews of her beauty and acting led to the previously mentioned role opposite James Cagney in *Kiss Tomorrow Goodbye*. About her performance in that film, a *New York Times* article stated, "As the moll, a superbly curved young lady [named] Barbara Payton performs as though she's trying to spit a tooth – one of the few Mr. Cagney leaves her." Despite the positive notices, Warner Brothers (WB) began casting Payton in small roles in undistinguished Westerns like *Dallas* and *Only The Valiant*. Part of the reason for this may have been that Payton was getting negative publicity for associating with real life gangsters and for raucous partying. To punish Payton for her "wild" ways, WB production chief Jack Warner assigned her a tiny role in a mediocre film. She refused it and he placed her on suspension. He took her off suspension to turn her over to independent producer Jack Broder to film *Bride of the Gorilla*. O'Dowd comments, "Although it was meant to be yet another act of punishment, the loan out was actually an unintentional blessing as it would provide Barbara with the second of two films for which she will forever be known."

Payton was engaged to A-list actor Franchot Tone when working on *Bride*. During production, she met B-list actor Tom Neal, best known for the acclaimed film noir *Detour*, and became strongly enamored of him. Payton shuffled back and forth between the two men. Finally, a confrontation led to a physical fight between the two males – one oddly resembling that between Barney and Klaas over Dina in *Bride*. Like Klaas, Tone was lean; like Barney, Neal heavily muscled. Neal battered Tone into a coma. Luckily, Tone survived and recovered. Payton married Tone.

However, within months, she returned to Neal. Much of the public turned against Payton and Neal who appeared in low-budget films for a few years and then found themselves unable to get movie work. Payton's last movie, *Murder Is My Beat*, was released in 1955. By the time her final film was made, her relationship with Neal, whom she never married, had ended. Neal left the film industry for landscaping. In 1965, he shot and killed wife Gail. He was convicted of manslaughter, and served six years in prison. Paroled in 1971, he died six months later.

Depressed by being blacklisted from the motion picture industry, Payton became an alcoholic prostitute. Her price slid as she lost her looks, going from a curvaceous beauty to a bloated, toothless hag. The enviable waistline in *Bride* became a potbelly distended by liver disease. She died of liver failure in 1967 at the age of 39. The devastation of her life is reminiscent of the devastation of Van Gelder Manor in *Bride*.

Cheesy, cheap, camp, thoroughly entertaining, remarkably well acted, and oddly meaningful, *Bride of the Gorilla* well deserves its cult film status.

Bibliography

Bride of the Gorilla (1951).
    http://www.imdb.com/title/tt0043360.
Bride of the Gorilla on ALLMovie.
    http://www.msn.com/en-ca/movies/movie/bride-of-the-gorilla/AA4ejIh.
Bride of the Gorilla (1951). Cult Movie Reviews.
    http://princeplanetmovies.blogspot.com/2008/12/bride-of-gorilla-1951.html?zx=7ef5417b57436ce3.
Bride of the Gorilla (1951). Movie Mis-Treatments.
    http://www.movie-mistreatments.com/Bride%20of%20the%20Gorilla.html.
O'Dowd, John. *Kiss Tomorrow Goodbye: The Barbara*

Payton Story. BearManor Media. 2006.

Shamout, Omar. "'Bride of the Gorilla' in Classic Cool Context." http://www.kcet.org/shows/classic_cool_theater/web-extras/bride-of-the-gorilla-in-classic-cool-context.html.

Terkelsen, Edward Larsen. "Bride of the Gorilla." *The Film Palace*. May 3, 2005. http://www.thefilmpalace.com/bride_of_the_gorilla.htm.

ARTICLE

Polyvagal theory:
a Potentially Unifying Conceptual Framework for Paranormal Experiences
R.D. Hayes

It was 2002. I was living in Houston, TX, a city of approximately 4 million people, with my girlfriend and our new baby while working as a postdoctoral fellow at a basic research lab at the medical school, located in one of the eleven hospitals of the Texas Medical Center. Between patients, visiting family members, and employees, probably 100,000 people came and went from those facilities every day.

I was tired, all the time. The baby was in daycare, catching every cold in town, and was sick almost constantly for about six months (which in time would result in an unusually competent immune system, so that those minor illnesses are now quite rare). This kept me and my girlfriend up in shifts, so we were both sleep-deprived. She drove to Clear Lake every day, to the Barnes & Noble across the street from NASA's Johnson Space Center. I walked or biked to the medical center every day from our first apartment on Shepherd Ave down through the campus of Rice University. This was six or seven days every week. Our Canadian postdoc and her husband each got six months of parental leave when they had a baby, but my wife's Fortune 500 corporate job gave her only six weeks, and as a father I got nothing. Again, this was 2002. Things have shifted slightly since then, in terms of work culture.

One night, about 2am, I was awakened by a loud metallic banging coming from the baby's room. This woke the baby, who began screaming. I jumped out of bed in my underwear and made my way to the door of the baby's room. As I arrived, the window air conditioner tore loose from the window frame and fell out the window to hang, still running, by its thick power cord. The person who had been jumping up and down on the air conditioner fell past the window to the ground below. From my elevated position inside the apartment I could see three or four heads silhouetted by streetlights out in the darkness of the alleyway.

I started to move into the room and was surprised to find that my muscles wouldn't work. I was stuck in the doorway. I pushed, mentally, and only succeeded in tiny postural shifts. My hands (on the doorframe?) and my feet wouldn't move at all. The baby was screaming even louder now.

The people outside sounded like young males. It occurred to me that I needed to at least say something. I tried to open my mouth. That worked, a little bit, but I couldn't exhale at first. After several tries I got a sort of breathy wheeze, which gradually strengthened into screamed vowels. I could not control my lips enough to shape consonants.

I grew up reading comics and watching Lou Ferrigno on *The Incredible Hulk*, and suddenly I realized that my voice was the only weapon that I had. If they came in through the window, I was in no condition to fight them, and the screaming baby in the corner would be in danger. So I **roared**, like the Hulk. I threw my breath at them, squeezing down on the intercostal muscles of the rib cage, over and over. It started high and small, but with each breath it grew until I was moving towards the window. I still couldn't make words. The sounds I was making were not speech, which depends on the cerebral cortex, the newest parts of the human brain. They were more like animal cries, from somewhere deeper.

The boys, or teens, or whatever, jumped and ran away, possibly laughing. I couldn't tell because I couldn't feel or hear anything but "the raging spirit that dwells within." I leaned out the window and hurled my voice after them, venting that rage until it left me, and I could breathe and move more normally, and I could begin soothing the baby, who was hot and red with screaming, too. I hurt my vocal cords. They were sore for days.

***

The testimony above would sound very familiar to many paranormal investigators, with a few differences. Temporary paralysis features in many stories. Most often the victim is asleep and awakes to find a malevolent presence in the room, either seen near the bed, or felt sitting on the victim's chest, pressing down and preventing the victim from breathing. This classic form of sleep paralysis is thought to be due to a partially failed transition from REM sleep to waking. During REM (Rapid Eye Movement) sleep, when most remembered dreams take place, the skeletal muscles are paralyzed by the inhibitory neurotransmitter glycine acting on the motor neurons in the spinal cord. This normal paralysis prevents us from acting out our dreams and injuring ourselves or our loved ones, as comedian Mike Birbiglia famously did when he jumped through the closed second-story window of a hotel while sleepwalking. Both sleepwalking and sleep paralysis are included in a large group of sleep-related disorders called **parasomnias**.

I experienced this type of classic sleep paralysis one time, as a teenager. I did see something in the corner of my room. However, the form it took was not a Shadow Man with glowing eyes, but Elvis Presley in a white sequined jumpsuit, with inky black tentacles of hair that thrashed chaotically above his head and then reached for me in a rush, the shock of which snapped me out of that state. I interpreted this, then and now, not as a supernatural visitation but as a momentary continuation of a dream image into waking consciousness.

My doorway experience in Houston, on the other hand, did not occur until I was already up and moving. I have no personal or family history of sleepwalking. This particular moment of paralysis seems to have had more in common with the work of Stephen Porges, currently a professor at the University of North Carolina at Chapel Hill. Among other researchers, he has extended discussion of the classic "fight or flight" responses — both of which depend on adrenaline from the sympathetic nervous system — to include a "freeze" response, which depends more on a different transmitter, acetylcholine, from the parasympathetic nervous system.

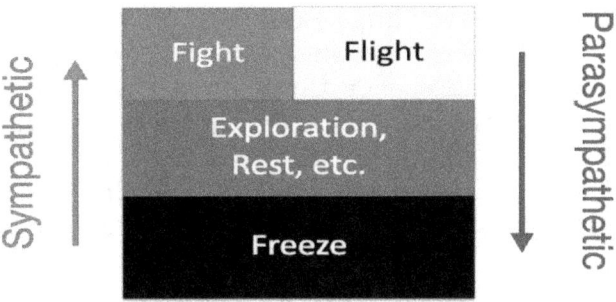

Figure 1. *A summary of Porges's polyvagal theory. The involuntary autonomic nervous system contains two main branches. The sympathetic system, using adrenaline, pushes "up," increasing alertness and mobilizing energy stores for quick emergency use. The parasympathetic system, using acetylcholine, pushes "down," calming body and mind, pushing energy towards rest and repair mechanisms. These two branches, in balance, produce normal exploratory behavior (aka "free will"). When one or the other dominates, behavior is pushed to involuntary extremes in the name of survival.*

Fight-or-flight responses occur in response to threats that might be effectively dealt with in either of those ways, meaning threats where the opponents are somewhat evenly matched. Overwhelming threats, however — threats that can be neither fought nor fled, the stuff of much horror media — often trigger freezing or fainting responses, especially in cold-blooded creatures like reptiles and amphibians, as well as in mammals with small brains like rodents. Most famously, the Virginia opossum, with its small brain and low body temperature, can "play dead" in this state for hours, during which it is not conscious and supposedly feels no pain, not even from bites or broken bones. "Fainting" goats are another example, one which was originally a spontaneous mutation, but which now is deliberately maintained by humans through selective breeding.

Humans have huge and hungry brains, which consume about 20% of the calories we eat, despite weighing only a little over three pounds. This is more than any other animal on Earth. We cannot survive for long with reduced blood flow, except under special circumstances like low temperatures. Humans therefore tend to undergo a large range of **partial** freeze responses that are lumped together as "dissociative" states, with highly variable effects on perception, memory, and behavior.

To use a real-world metaphor, imagine a rolling brownout such as those that plagued western power grids in the early 2000s. The effects of these partial power outages were highly unpredictable, depending on which machines were starved for electricity in each particular case. My personal combination of relatively clear verbal thought and complete but temporary bodily paralysis in the testimony above is only one of many, many possibilities.

Polyvagal theory was named for the vagus nerve (Latin for "wanderer") because it innervates all the vital organs, collecting information about almost everything happening in the body. Porges's work could likewise serve as a unifying conceptual framework for the incredible diversity of paranormal experiences.

Author's Note: *The 1978 television version of* The Incredible Hulk *had much more in common with modern paranormal media than with the super-heroics of the Marvel Cinematic Universe. For instance, the words* **monster**, **creature**, *and* **sightings** *were used regularly in describing the Hulk, and Jack McGee, the "investigative reporter" who followed the Hulk's sporadic trail of destruction was generally considered a crackpot. McGee was an especially humorless version of his equally* *obnoxious fictional predecessor Carl Kolchak, subject of a previous article for this magazine.*

REFERENCES / FURTHER READING

Cassidy, Theodore C. (1978). Opening narration for *The Incredible Hulk*. CBS Television.
https://www.youtube.com/watch?v=0o_k5X9CV0k
Gray, Adam, and Gray, Andrew (2018). *The Nightmare*. Paradocs Films.
https://www.graybrothersfilms.com/the-nightmare
Birbiglia, Mike (2012). *Sleepwalk with Me*. Bedrock Media, WBEZ Chicago. Coincidentally, he also compared himself to the Hulk.
https://www.stephenporges.com/

www.ingramcontent.com/pod-product-compliance
Lightning Source LLC
LaVergne TN
LVHW012027060526
838201LV00061B/4494